THE BATTLE WITHIN

What if your inner voice took control?

Romaine Davidson

THE BATTLE WITHIN

Romaine Davidson was born in the town of St. Kathrine, Jamaica and studied Mechanical Engineering throughout College and the University of Bristol UK. He is Married and currently lives in London.

In Memory of the ones that lost the battle to their voice.

TABLE OF CONTENT

PROLOGUE

The feeling twisted and pulled in my stomach as the pen formed words from the heart. Sometimes I like to get away from the pace of life in the city. I like this field and this bench where I am now sat; it is where my grandparents used to take me on the weekends, and it brings memories of joy as a child. "I love you Grandma and Granddad" I murmur as a gush of wind travels through the follicles of my hair causing a warm sensation in my stomach. The open air of magical colours, sprawling valleys with beautiful flowers and green grass accompany me.

"It was a great day at work" I continue to write in my diary. "Mr Sam and Miss Kate in particular was the highlight of my day. This is a letter to my future self, a letter of hope and aspiration. I long for a child, one I could love as pure as I do Andreas, his love for me takes away all fear and pain, his security is that of three hundred soldiers." I take a break from writing to view a magpie chasing the other and in the distance others walk.

"I've worked at the care home for some time now. Occasionally I meet some interesting people. I chuckle to my giddy self as I remember a time Miss Kate told a story of how she met her soul mate, a true gentle soul," I concluded.

Old Sam has been asking me if I'm happy. I know I'm happy. Despite all the challenges I always have the strength to carry on, but Andreas com-

pletes me. I know he is struggling right now but I will always be there for him. I turn my attention away from the memories and notice an elderly man in a wheel chair is being pushed down the field towards me.

There is a young boy beside him - no more than ten years old. Perhaps a little older. He holds a ball in his hand. When they get close to me they smile and I smile back.

"Your Grandpa?" I ask the boy.

"Yes," he says.

I end the brief encounter with a smile that warms me, hugging my body like the comfort of a freshly washed jumper. They walk off into the distance and my mind wonders, thinking of whether they are OK. The sun begins to fade and time is going.

I need to get back.

The street lights are on all over as I gaze out the window of the bus. "Perhaps Andreas is not back yet," I wonder as I press the bell and begin a descend down the stairs. "But then his evening plans are rather unpredictable, and he could be hanging out with Rob," I end by saying.

"Hello, Nicole," Elise greets me as I get closer to the bottom stair.

"Hello, Elise," I respond, rather surprised.

"The teenage girl in Number Eight," she said. "Her mother is sick."

"Oh no! She lives alone with her mother, doesn't she?"

"Yes, she does."

"Dear God! Where is she? All alone in the house?"

"No, I'm looking out for her until her aunt comes to help out."

"That's very kind of you, Elise. I'll pass by and see how she's doing."

I walk with Elise to her door and we walk in. The girl is sitting on a sofa, staring vacantly at the TV. She must be sixteen or so. The room is in a mess that matches her current situation. So young, I say to myself. Her name is Claire.

"Hello Claire," I greet as I sit beside her, taking her hand and noticing how particularly soft they are. "Your mother will be fine," I whisper, wishing to take away her pain. I can see that she has been crying, and the signs of grief and the unthinkable cloud her eyes.

She stares at me and nods slowly.

"You'll be fine love," I repeat, and she hugs me as if she wants to say thank you.

It is past eight PM when I finally leave to go to my apartment. By then Claire is asleep, mercifully.

Andreas is sitting facing the already turned off TV when I walked in, and he turns. His eyes brightens.

"For some reason I recall the first day I saw Andreas. My intention was to be a friend – to give him a shoulder to lean on. He seemed like a troubled man. From the moment I saw him I knew he was kind, harmless and a loving soul: Our friendship developed into the most loving relationship." I picked up the pen again and concluded the chapter in my diary with a simple phrase. "My life has changed."

I put my diary on the bed side table and stand staring at Andreas as he sits there. I have a feeling that he is fighting an invisible battle. One he won't share with me. The best I can do is wait and hope he'll talk to me. I tried yesterday to get him to open up without success. But whatever it is he is going through seems to have frightened him. He seems like a man facing something beyond his imagination – beyond his worst fear. He seems like a trapped man.

CHAPTER 1

The clock above the fridge read just past midnight.

I'm usually in bed by now, but tonight was unusual, it was only a couple hours since the lights in the flat went out. The whole block was a victim to the darkness and the sound of shuffling and scrambles for candles was evidently clear.

"Get the torch in the cupboard by the scissors! HURRY!" was the cry from our neighbour. We chuckled with humour- Nicole and I; this was our first-time experiencing a power blackout - was I scared or anxious? Erm, I don't think so.

Minutes ticked by, and still there was no light. Nicole was asleep on the couch as I sat beside her, but I couldn't close my eyes for one reason or another. I was tired from a long day at work listening to the sound of my boss shouting and screaming at the fact that the deadline was close and the presentation was not yet ready. The denial in his tone suggested self-guilt and we all blamed him. Now I lay on the couch trying to catch some sleep, but something or someone kept my eyes from closing.

The power had wiped out our usual distractions, no wifi, no radio, no tel-lie-vision, and the sound of heavy raindrops battering the roofs and cars sounded louder than they normally would. I wanted to believe that it was the rain that kept me awake but its sound was in fact a sweet melody to my ears, though at times it resembled a creepy horror movie.

The clock ticked on, 3a.m. Now my neck was hurting, a result of the constant pressure of supporting my dozing and swaying head. My eyes were losing the battle to stay open, but they opened instantly when I heard the eerie sound of feet on the floor boards of the creaky stairs.

No one ever comes to this block, especially at this time.

My eyes were no longer heavy as I nervously wondered. Strange voices came to my ears from outside the door, and it sounded as if a discussion or argument was in full swing. Were we about to be robbed? What type of weapon did these unwelcome night lurkers carry with them? Gun? Knife? I wondered, with my heart in my mouth, it pounded, raced, and the apprehension could be heard through the whistling of my lips.

Nicole was still fast asleep. My beloved, loving, loyal Nicole. The apple of my eye and my inseparable fiancée. She is as loyal to me as I am to her. I could never imagine the future without her standing by my side. If my mind travelled to a time ten years from now and I was standing in the yard of our suburban house, then she was right there by my side while the cool breeze graced our faces and the unison of birds was our banquet. She was as much a part of my future as she was of my present. I knew it in my heart. If every friend I ever had decided to turn away, Nicole would be the one left standing by my side.

I shone a torch through the keyhole.

The eyes of the intruders peered through the hole in the door, and it startled me to a dramatic jump - as if a spider was near. My heart skipped a beat. The hole was only the size of a key, the eyes had powers in them, the hollow grey pupils was the give away. I was able to observe that much: each time it blinked it eased the melting of my skin; it was fiery, peppery and it scorched. I breathed a sigh of relieve each time it blinked, then it opened again to continue the torment. My breathing increased with every gasp of air I searched for and it sounded like a panic.

I shouted without alarming her: "They see my every move, and it frightens me." I trembled in fear. I could taste their intentions as I whispered for fear of being heard, and so I searched her eyes with the hope that she would offer some kind of support, but she was still dead to the world. My voice deepened as I said in a stern tone: "They are bad people, they smell of trouble, trouble I didn't commit. I'm afraid Nicole, they're going to get me. Please don't let them get me Nicole, please".

"Andreas!" the voice shouted. It was patronising and soft, direct and clear. It continued, "I knew your parents, I knew their voices, I knew their touch, I felt their kisses on my cheeks." The voice got deeper and the room instantly chilled.

The sound of rain had disappeared out of range. Strangely, it was as if the droplets had been carried away by the dark clouds, one by one they travelled to another poor soul, the focal point of my ears are now his. I couldn't see him but I pictured him clean-shaven – so curiously crisp and smooth that it only made him all the more sinister. I began to nudge Nicole to get up but the voice continued, "The night of the fire I was there with you, don't you remember?" he shouted with a vehement tone. I looked at Nicole, wondering if she heard, but she hadn't. He began to whisper, "We spoke of a plan, a plan to keep a little secret, don't you remember you fool?" his voice escalated, this time with sharp anger on his lips. His voice shot up again as he repeated the question, "Oh, what a shame!" he said with disgust. He remained there the whole time as if his lips were chained to the door. "I am the one you feared for so long!" he barked. Frightened and shaken, I faded away, sneaked away from the encounter - or did he vanish? I wasn't sure, but thc voice had stopped.

CHAPTER 2

I woke up early that morning drenched from the heat of a typical July, the soaring headache and sore back suggesting little sleep, and the veins in my eyes bloody. Nicole had already left for work. Every morning no later than seven fifty-five she would be out that door, her breakfast prepared and her clothes ironed and spotless. She was quite the organiser, never late. This particular morning, I wondered many times what I would do to keep her around. Telling her what had happened might make her run away. I rolled out of bed and strolled into work that morning, confused at what had happened last night, afraid of the actual answer. Without moving my lips, I mimed, "Am I going crazy?"

I went through my normal routine. My students took their normal seats in their normal uninterested demeanour, the same normal conversations with fellow teachers took place and the whole day went by without hearing the voice in my head. I was glad, but still confused. *Maybe it was a dream*, or was that wishful thinking... Despite this feeling, I tried to carry on as normal – at least on the outside.

As the school day came to a close, a moment of relief exited my body, the voice hadn't shown his face and I was able to continue as normal. I was relaxed and jubilant as I left for the gym that evening.

It was 7.15 p.m. when I arrived. If the voice in my head had a body, it certainly wasn't visible to my eyes. Or this was just a really long nightmare.

I walked in through the revolving door.

The tang in the air was that of a diabetic foot. The gym was half-full and the smell was unexplainable; I mean, you get used to it after a while, but the initial greeting was never welcoming.

I had decided to meet up with Robin. As I walked in, the clock's big face and two arms on the wall read seven fifteen. I needed to regain some of my sanity so I called on my good friend Rob. Rob stood a little shorter than I am - he would say he's taller, but that's not the case; he has short legs, short torso and sometimes his left leg seems shorter than the right. He would call me fat and I would call him short, that's just how it was.

"Hello Rob," I would always say, and his typical greeting would always be "What's good?" in a throaty tone that resembled a growl. *I think he's trying to keep hold of his youth, he dresses way younger than a normal thirty-five year old should, his choice of words are parallel to that of a sixteen year old.* I looked at him on the exercise bike as his little feet tried to reach the peddles.

"Rob!" I shouted over the loud grunts of the weight lifters, "I have something really weird to ask you. Now, don't be alarmed, don't be extra, I just need an answer," I had to warn him; he can be a clown when it comes to serious issues - he's never serious.

"Sure, go ahead," he said with a smirk.

"Erm…" I hesitated, then I blurted it out, "do you ever hear voices, I mean, the voices that no one else but you can hear, or just a voice in your head?" I continued to explain. Rob took a moment to think about what exactly he was being asked.

"No," he replied, then paused and affirmed again, this time quite gingerly, "no, I don't think so," with a question mark in his tone.

Before he could get his last, slow words out I jumped in, annoyed at his diagnosis. "Well, it happened to me last night. I heard a voice, and in a gravelly tone he said he was there when my parents' house burnt down."

Rob paused his little legs from peddling, then questioned, "The night your parents died?"

"The voice also said he and I were planning it the whole time, like, what was he talking about? Repeating it shocked me more than the first time. I didn't understand it then and I don't understand it now." My eyes started to water and Rob laid his heavy hand on my shoulder. The session ended uncompleted.

There was a mixture of concern and puzzlement in Rob's eyes as I walked out of the gym. He would probably have been amused if I hadn't mentioned my dead parents. He must have realised that I wasn't in one of my joking moods. I walked purposefully along the pavement, my eyes scanning the passing traffic for a cab, intending to end this day as normal as possible.

The clouds in the sky formed a black hive as the mood was now dull and dry. The moon light shone through the cracks of the hive, exposing a glimmer of hope, abnormal sounds rung my ears that evening and I was afraid of being lonely. I roared out in response, but no sound came out. That day was the first time in a long while that fear hugged me and wouldn't let go.

The keys in my pocket jingled as I reached the top of the stairs. I opened the front door. Nicole was on the couch, her favourite place after a long day's work. She was snuggled up with the teddy bear I got her for Valentine's day. The corridor was scented with the sweet smell of caramel candles, and in the backdrop of the scent was the whiff of cooked carrots or cooked peas, maybe both. The hallway layered with our most precious memories and moments. I glanced at one in particular - the smallest one on a large wall. Ah, that was the evening we went on a lunch date, I recalled; the food was horrible but the drinks saved the date. Nicole insisted that we take photos but I didn't want to, as usual. Snap, went the camera's flash, exposing her inability to hear my insecurity even as my face twisted and my eyes were falling out. That was all the camera caught as I tried to turn away, but she got me. I smiled and we both laughed at the crises the whole day had brought. *This wall will forever be my sanctuary, a few seconds stop here will always make me happy*

I continued in to greet her. It was late, maybe past ten.

"Andreas," a faint voice vocalised.

I scurried through my head for an identity. At first I thought it was Nicole, but the voice was too manly. I replied with confusion in my eyes, but with a deep bearish growl, the voice shouted: "You mean to tell me you still don't know who I am? Come on, Andreas!"

The words help me rested as a prisoner behind my teeth; I tried to get it to her ears but their freedom was already taken and I trembled like a cold winter's night as my body and mind shut down. She looked at me for clarification, but I struggled to find the right rhythm; whatever was leaving my lips wasn't words, just mere sounds of muddle. I slowed down, drew in as much air as my lungs could hold. Nervous as I was, the words started to make sense as I explained how scared I was, embarrassed and still frightened at the prospect of summoning that thing.

"What thing?" she demanded for an answer. I went on. I was able to explain in that very short moment that feeling of loneliness, loss and fear that concealed me. She comforted me with a hug, opening her ears as she heard my cry. It made me feel wholesome that someone wanted me. I wasn't sure if she understood how I felt, but her embrace was enough. I felt connected once again; I felt safe, my face lit up with delight. She suggested I seek help and she even offered to find it for me, but I declined with embarrassment as the idea of someone finding out that I was going crazy wasn't an option. I hated the idea; besides, I don't like people, I reminded her, I wanted to help myself.

"What is it about people and society that gets under your skin so much?" she asked.

"Ohm, I don't know; is it because people are like water with their ability to be shaped by any and everything, or maybe it feels like the world itself is one big scam fuelled by consumption, propaganda messages at every turn? Or the fact that all our heroes are a bunch of liars hiding behind the perfect image, our social media fantasy as a virtual escape? Just a bunch of cowards; no one lives any more, no one has the time to love or be loved any more, that's what disappoints me." I looked in her eyes and noticed that I was going too deep; I realised that she didn't like hearing what I was saying, and it seemed as though every time she asked a question she hoped for a different answer - after all, she was the complete opposite to me, she loved the world and hoped the best for it. I was not convinced that the voice would go away and it frightened me.

Nicole went to bed soon after; she graced in her silk black gown, she kissed me goodnight as she asked when I'd be joining her, but I stayed up staring at the screen I despised so much, with one elbow leaning on the arm rest. A strange feeling travelled up my spine as I entertained the thought of a connection with this voice. I wanted to know who the voice belonged to: was it my father or could it be mine? I can vaguely remember a voice that played in my head as a child - it was always a nice voice and we laughed together, played together and became good friends, as if we were one.

The moon was the only thing keeping the sky company; the cats and dogs ruled the streets at that hour. It was poetic to see it as I stood at the kitchen window and stared out at it. The voice had returned and this time he was laughing; an evil slow gravelly laugh.

"Why are you laughing?" I asked.

"You are starting to remember me," he pointed out abruptly. "Do you not remember you was the one that caused the fire?"

"The fire," I repeated in a low distressed tone.

"Do you not remember the way Spider-man melted, the way it spread across the living room?" he continued to bombard me with questions I knew nothing about. I needed him out my head.

"What if I'm right?" he concluded. "What if you need to pay for what you did?" he asked. "Sure, I whispered in your ear to burn his face and you listened, and burning your parents alive was the outcome. I hope you are proud of that," he continued, "I hope you live the rest of your life in regret and I hope you die with this on your chest."

"Stop!" I cried out, "stop, stop," I said but no sound left my mouth. The fire was burning in my head and it was painful. The conversation heated up, my fingers wrapped round the follicles of my head as I tugged and pulled, my eyes widened as I searched the galaxy; it was empty. I looked crazy, I sounded insane, and if anyone were to see me they would call an ambulance, and that's being generous - a straight jacket would be appropriate.

With a sigh, I stepped away from the window. The blissful lamp in the sky would not help me stay calm – not with his voice in my head. Neither would it help me to snap to reality – the reality where voices exist for the purpose of subconscious guidance. I stared around the kitchen, and sat my weary body on the seat at the kitchen table. Here Nicole and I had sat and laughed; here I had sat and watched her move gracefully around the kitchen. He had no right to invade my house, the places that held great memories and tarnish them with his unwelcome stature.

In a fit of anger, I slammed my hand on the table where we dined that same night. I slammed it again, and this time it dented the table, bruised my hand, and in that moment, Nicole woke up. She took the corner of the corridor like an F1 car and came racing to the living room. I looked up at her as she looked down on me, I laid on the floor like a flat frog trying to cross the road, with my fingers still tangled in my thick hair.

"Andreas," she cried out, "what is the matter?" she worriedly repeated. No sound came from my mouth and no words left my lips. She dragged me up as if I had been shot and then held me. She cried with me as her strength resurrected the strength in my numb legs, fear navigated itself from my being to hers, as the panic in her became real. It was evident as I felt her heart beat punching my chest. I saw the mirror conveniently placed behind the sofa and I slammed my eyes shut, unable to look at myself. I reopened them, whispering in a faint but clear voice, "All I see is shame, fear and disgust. I hate it," I screamed falling flat once again. She crumbled with me this time. We sat on the floor while the motion of rocking calmed me and she held me tight and rocked me steady, and then asked if I remembered the night of the proposal. She went on to bring me back to that moment

"Andreas," she whispered faintly, almost seducing me. Her breath was warm and it travelled the length of my body. "Do you remember how beautiful the place looked? Do you remember the laughs we had?" her face beamed a smile. "Do you remember that night, Andreas?"

"Yes," I replied with tears rolling down the mountain of my cheeks. She spoke of the encounter: "The place was extra beautiful. I remember you said you didn't see anything different, wasn't sure if you were being serious, your face was serious as a plank, you referred to it as an old beautiful place, and I liked that. That place brought us so much laughter and spice that night; the creamy off-white, box-shaped building, a dozen windows welcomed the delicious sunshine on a bright sunny day, warm moonlight entertained us that evening. Atop sits three orange chimneys that look like cannons never been fired, Andreas" She paused. I stared at her and then continued to gaze across the room, not really focusing on anything but resuscitating that amazing evening along with her. As she spoke the scenes replayed in my mind, and it was as if we were back in time enjoying that evening again. "Do you remember those horrid chimneys?" A nod was returned. "Protruding out the side is a balcony overlooking the canal, it reflected a distorted image of the spot. The canal was filled with leaves from the ingrown trees etched in the mouldy bridge, the entrance is glass fronted and lively, inside you are welcomed by warm blue and gold neon lights, stimulated by faint jazz playing in the background - Miles Davis I think it was. Gold top counters with candles lit all around, a step back from the bar you had tables and booths running along the windows decorated with roses in an opaque flower jar which looked out at the canal and soothed us by its slow-moving river. A modern-looking block of flats sits further down the canal freshly-painted; you can still taste it in the air.

'Can I take your orders,' the waiter interrupted. Babes do you remember that?" she said, breaking the story to share the moment of impoliteness.

"A glass of rose," I told her. "the intrusion was rude and I wasn't happy, but I wanted the drink. I think he knew I wasn't amused and I could see it in his face. He then turned and asked you, 'and for you sir?' in his posh plummy tone. It didn't make sense; he spoke like an English prince but was a waiter.

And now I may as well have been the one telling this story. We were in sync as she narrated the events of the evening as clear as a video tape, and my thoughts were in sync with every word she spoke, as if there was a pen writing on the walls of my mind, bringing memories back into sharp focus.

'A pint of Guinness' you uttered, suppressing the laughter. Your compliments was touching, you looked beautiful, you said - it caught me by surprise. You waited until I had the glass to my lips, you sneaky." I looked down on him still in a state on the floor, his soft lips widened, exposing a beautiful set of teeth. I looked around the darkness of the room, searching for a light to give him. I continued the motion to sooth him as I would a baby in my arms, as I continued, "You had a look on your face as if you had a cun-

ning plan. 'The way that black dress fits so luxuriously to your soft silky frame' you said in a joking tone, that's exactly how you said it," I whispered it to him. I wasn't sure if he had fallen asleep at this point, but there was no snoring so I continued to rock. The way you wear that red lipstick on those delicious lips,' she giggled again, 'I love you until the very end' I remembered word for word.

My eyes watered at this point. thank you my love, I replied; my tongue was twisted, I was dumb for words - your words have always been such magic to my ears. She moved her body to sound of the music playing in her head, it was the background jazz from the bar, and before I could get another word out, you said don't say anything else, do you remember that part, do you remember shutting me up, I asked. He said nothing, his palms pressed firmly against his ears, so that no sound was to penetrate. My body trembled – I know you was in such state, and there was nothing I could do; I wanted to call my sister, but my phone was in the other room and I didn't want to leave you, so I continued to search the room for that light, but only the moon presented itself. I remember you in your handsome black suit, white shirt with no tie, I remember you looking so smart, tall, dark and tasty, I love the way your dreamy hazelnut eyes swallowed me in, I love the way your sturdy hands made me feel safe, that night you held me like a knight in shining armour. I want you to soak up all the attention tonight; you continued, saying these strange things, and I was confused. Could you not see the way my eyebrow closed in, you was up to something and I didn't know what, then the waiter returned with our meal, interrupting the moment, thank you, we both replied.

The night went on, you looked at your watch and it was just after eleven; the atmosphere had picked up, well-dressed ladies and gentlemen spilled into the bar, ready to wine and dine their partners, and have a good time. The spot became full pretty quickly, and many more couples filled the tables, hiding the beautiful gold tops, many more conversations popped off, the music got louder as people filled the dance floor, turning it into a rave, we bumped and squeezed our way through the crowd as we exited, and walked along the canal fingers entwined. I closed my eyes, taking a picture with my eyelids, like a photographer shutters, making sure it would never be forgotten. The night was nice and warm, it was your idea to walk home, as we stepped out into the realm of all possibilities, we slowed our pace to savour the moment, as we reached the end of the canal you pointed out a poster on the side of a building, it read, "Let your voice be heard." We thought nothing of it at the time but now it makes sense. Still unresponsive. I checked to see if he was breathing; Andreas, I whispered, could this have been a sign? Could this have been someone warning you about something - we saw this only a couple days ago. I don't know, he replied lazily without a movement in his limbs; I repeated, it was as if someone was trying to say something to you.

He shrugged it off as a means to nothing, and we continued to walk as we talked, with the moonlight gleaming on us like a spotlight on a stage, and in a flash of a clap you spun me around in a swift motion of salsa brilliance, looked deep into my eyes, fell to one knee and said: " will you marry me"? In that moment it seems as though the whole world had stopped, the earth wasn't moving, people had been stopped to be our audience, the dogs stopped barking, and as you waited for an answer, I shouted, YES, YES, YES. It was at the moment that I realised what true happiness felt like; you smiled from ear to ear as I picked you up by your chin, kissed you softly with tears trickling down my cheeks. You've made me the happiest woman on this planet, I uttered with a trembling lip, and a watery nose. We embraced with a further hug and kiss, and we continued to our home. "would you like to come up for coffee?"

I joked. "Most definitely," you replied with a big smile on your face, knowing what was to come; the mood was set, everything was going perfect. You had this planned all day while I was at work, I asked like a detective homing in on her culprit, I stepped through the front door, greeted at the door by petals of red and white roses - what was to follow was moments of passion, she concluded.

"You see Andreas, you need to get back to times like these; these are the times and feelings that will give you peace again. Try to fight this and hang in there, get back to your normal life," I repeated lovingly, "I will be with you the whole way through."

CHAPTER 3

The next morning, I rang into work sick. I didn't know what was wrong with me but I knew I was not right. The female voice on the other end of the phone was stern, officer-like, and it sent a chill down my spine as if she could read and see me through the phone, hear my thoughts, see my pain. I hung the phone up before the customary bye was said. The side of my head was burning, as if I had rolled in a pepper field or someone had stood on it all night. I found myself slumped on the couch, curled up like a turtle in its shell, protected only by the thickness of the t-shirt that hugged my skin. The sound of sand paper dragged on the floor as Nicole entered the room. It was unusual of her to move like this; she only did things like that when she was torn between making a decision. My guess is, the thought of leaving me for work was the issue.

"Go," I said, hinting that I would love her regardless.

"Would you like to be alone?" she asked, stepping closer with suggestion of a pending hug. I replied with a pause and an artificial yes as I wiped the sweat dripping from my nose. I was sweating for some reason but didn't know why and I wanted my top off, but I would feel vulnerable and unprotected. I hated how I felt last night, turning to lay on my back, making sure my voice could be heard.

"You must go before you're late. I will be fine; you can call me later - I just need some rest." She travelled her long nails down my right arm as she walked towards the door; it felt sensual, but it was the wrong time, instead it made me weary.

I began to rummage through the internet, each click taking me deeper and deeper into a world of a specialist. I was afraid to be diagnosed and I was uneasy. I got up, I sat down - I was in a mess, but I knew I had to continue, so I filled the search bar with the words "voice in my head." The results lit up like a fireworks display as all sorts of documents came back; notes, videos, it was all there, testimonials, it was all there. I was relieved and scared at the same time. *I now have a path to cure this thing*, I thought.

I eased back into the couch thinking of the X-Men movie, then I thought of mutants, then I thought of me - am I one? Nah, I whispered as the air left my cheeks.

I continued to scroll into the unknown: split personality, bi-polar, depression, schizophrenia all kept popping up, and they all pointed to mental issues. My heart began to race at the reality and I slammed the laptop shut. There was a moment of silence, a pause, and the only thing that was present was the thumping of my heart beat. *I can't be mental*, I began to whisper over and over again, and each time it got louder and louder. "It doesn't fit me," I shouted, "what if this society has gotten it all mixed up and backwards, what if the so-called crazy ones are the ones of love, reason and conscience, what if we as a people have gotten it all wrong and are silencing humanities' answers?" I stood up, looked in the mirror and whispered, *I'm not crazy*.

Where was the line between sanity and insanity? The inner voice – we all hear it. Does insanity begin when that voice becomes too loud? Or when that voice begins to control us? I needed to find the line between sanity and insanity.

I reopened the laptop and read some more; it was more of the same.

I searched for the window in need of fresh air. *Are you sure you want to go outside*, the familiar voice returned, *they're going to get you he continued to taunt*. I told him to shut up and wedged my two fingers where the sound was coming from. My body now reddened with hate and anger and I unbolted the front door. Suspiciously I leaned forward to glance around the corner and the voice laughed a wicked laugh - he was mocking me; he knew he had my number marked, and sadly I knew it too. He smelt victory, and he was homing in on it.

"Andreas, Andreas," my neighbour called. Frightened at the surprise, and frankly the volume, I jumped in fear.

"Good morning, how are you doing?" flew out of his mouth.

"I'm fine," I responded with great precision and a lack of honesty. My upper lip trembled: that was the moment to confide in someone, to connect, to seek help. I waved him goodbye and speedily walked towards the bus stop. Whenever I saw this man, I would always refer to him as the old man; no one bothered to ask his name, and to be honest I didn't give him the time of my day. I blame the conformities of life, the busyness, I sighted.

I planted my feet on 337 bus towards the Albion Park and sat in my seat, my head hanging down to the floor as I pondered and entertained the idea of being alone, isolated in this world without anyone to comfort me, reassure me, without Nicole to love me. I turned my head in anguish as the feeling of defeat circled around me. I feared it and I must fight to prevent it.

The sound of a hungry baby cried as her mother fed her. I looked at the two of them and smiled, wishfully gazing. I closed my eyes for a moment; the moment felt long, but it was just enough time for me to picture my life this way. I longed for a family, a family I could call mine - *I mean Nicole is my family but I want a child, someone to cry for my attention, someone to run to the door as I come in from work, a boy* - I thought fanatically as the gaze turned into a stare, then a smile. I broke eye contact with the realm of possibilities and brought myself back to reality; it wasn't long before a voice greeted me with laughter. It was mean, like playground kids bickering, then it got rough and thunderous enough to make any house shake, let alone a shell like mine. He asked me the most wicked and evil question: "Do really think you can get that? You think they will allow you to be happy?" his voice escalated. "I don't think so," bringing his tone to an all-time high. He seemed upset, like I had done something to him, but I was innocent. I asked him, "Is it you that is denying me of my dreams or is it the ones you call them? Who are you?" I raised my voice, trying to return that same fright I received, not loud, but harsh enough to look crazy. The lady and the baby jumped and the scream got louder, and she turned and looked at me like I was something strange, a piece of dirt dragged for days and weeks. It was like she could smell a foul smell, like it wasn't normal, except in a place like London, it was normal. I rolled my eyes, embarrassed, but I got off at the next stop and walked. "I'm your inner being," the voice continued proudly, "the side of you that does what is necessary," he added in a terrible tone. His voice was always sharp, like a sound distortion from a microphone. "I've been in your head from the beginning and I will never go away. I know what you did," he taunted, "I know what you did."

The park created a contrast between itself and the backdrop of the city noises, and that is exactly what I wanted or maybe needed. Here i was able to reflect and shut out the the pressures of my dreams, expectations and responsibilities of the world. Here there was no TV screen, no distraction – just people seeking the bliss of relaxation and completeness. Here I could try to find sanity away from the noisy insanity of my home.

My legs turned. Freakishly confused, weak and tired, I planted myself on a bench in the park. I wanted to find out what this thing was talking about. I didn't ask him his name, I didn't care, but it made me angry. I sat there thinking, *I was fine the other day, now here I am, typical*, I raged. I asked him what he meant. "What did I do?" I shouted, narrowing in, "leave me alone," I screamed again, "please," as my voice lowered. I remembered a paragraph that mentioned exercise this morning, I looked at my overweight stomach and sighed. I shoved that aside and started to move my legs, and faster and faster I picked the up the pace and was now running. My chest started to cramp from the inside, my lungs went into overtime. I had to stop, reducing myself to walking speed, to save my frame from falling i had to sit. "You big overweight baboon, you still don't get it, do you, you are weak and sad," he began to pummel me, "you hate society so much that you misunderstand hate for love, you fear loneliness instead of embracing solidarity. I don't hate you, Andreas, I just don't need you." My eyes widened when he said that. "You tolerate abuse from people, maybe that's why you hate. The abuse happened once, and I won't stand by and accept it, you don't have the pedigree to become like me, I will have to break you, you can't get rid of me, I'm the one that gets rid of you." I was up against the ropes as he battered me; he wasn't a total liar, I'll admit. I had to compose myself, speechless, and no other words left my lips.

My defeated stature was filled with holes, not by a gun shot or a knife stab, but by the words that sunk so deep it was hard to walk straight. My shadow seemed to have gotten the message; it was nowhere to be found. I began to get anxious, which was something new to me. My future was unclear. "They are going to get me," I kept saying as my nails met the inside of my left arm with ferocious scraping. Blood was present on the underneath of my nails. My lazy feet took me to the main road; it was a busy afternoon. I had the urge to step out in front of one of the moving objects, but I listened instead. The ice cream van played a lullaby, the excited children laughed at the prospect of being flung up in the air by the swings, the last ten percent of battery took me out of the park and I headed in the direction of home. The fragrance of exhaust fumes swirled and lingered in my nostrils, the irritation causing a gush of air to blow out my nose. I hailed down a taxi that was luckily heading my way.

"Hey," I said as the car door closed and the atmosphere was quiet, "can you take me to bridge town street?" I was exhausted; I couldn't afford for him to say no, my legs couldn't take another step. I slumped deeper in his seat, almost sitting on the car floor. The driver gave me a gesture of acceptance along with a "sure."

"Tell the driver to speed up Andreas; he's going too slow, tell him now." Once again I plugged my ears, as if I was wearing one of those noise cancelling headphones, closing my eyes at the same time: if I can't hear nor see him, he's not there, I thought. The background made noises as if someone was talking. I removed my finger.

"Are you OK?" the driver asked. Afraid of the consequences, troubled with fear, tormented by someone - not that he was visible. "Driver," I whispered in the most polite of ways, "please can you slow down?" The temperature in my body raised as if the voice was angry. "Louder you fool, louder, he can't hear you, stop being so timid, stop being an idiot, just do as I say, you take orders from me so listen up. Tell the driver to speed up now," he repeated with a loud deafening tone. I opened my mouth but no sound materialised; louder he screamed. "Slow down," I uttered, disobeying his orders, "slow down please, I can't take this no more." The driver was in shock; I could sense him searching for his bible, readying his protection to what now seemed like an evil spirit. I felt his chair trembling; I was surprised that he didn't stop the car and kick me out, instead, my hands found themselves on the door handle, attempting to open it while the taxi was still in motion. The door was locked and unable to open and I sat back further in my seat, hoping to be swallowed up. My hand found my ears again, my eyes watered. "Are you ok back there, buddy?" this time a calm and softer voice asked. "We are almost at your stop," the driver notified with a worried look in the mirror.

"Are you going to answer the driver?" the voice troubled, "he wants to know what is wrong with you, you sound crazy right now." I removed my hands from my ear once again, placing it by my side for stability.

"Shut up," I fired back, trying to maintain some sort of strength, "you don't own me and mark my words I will be happy again, I will accomplish this, and you will leave me alone, for good. I don't believe anything you have said so far, you are a liar; now leave me alone." My phone started to ring; it was Nicole.

"Driver, you can let me off here,' I ordered. The driver obliged. I'd walk from here; I figured the fresh air would do me good. The energy returned to my legs; I called work not long after, hurried as the momentum of a small victory excited me; fresh start, I told them.

CHAPTER 4

I was out the tracks like a bullet from an already loaded gun, down the stairs, hopped and skipped past the last three creaking steps, slammed my palms against the door with all my might opening it, unleashing rays of light in my face, causing me to refocus my pupils. The bus I wanted was already at the stop readying to leave. My legs carried me fast, faster than a normal pace of walk, speed-walking I would say. As I began to increase the pace I ran. This time my hand was in the air, calling for the driver's attention, who I hoped was looking in his side mirror. I couldn't be late for work again - they already warned me. I dug deeper as if I was in the Olympic finals and ran; a sigh of relief left my nostrils as my feet reached the doors. *I made it,* my body thought. I took a seat to the rear of the packed bus, panting by this time as I tried to fill my lungs with air; it was difficult as the air was thick and rough. I needed to settle down before I collapsed. My phone rang, my fingers scurried around my body and bag until I located it. It was from Nicole. "Babes," she said in a hesitant and slow tone, "you've forgotten your lunch."

"Dammit," I called out in a soft bent out of shape tone. No one reacted to the sound. I was pleased: maybe because their ears were covered with headphones. I hurled my palm to my cheeks in annoyance; it wasn't a hard connection, but enough to make me adjust my cheeks in a swirly motion. "Aah, thanks," I said, dejected by that time, then hung up. "You stupid fool," I murmured, "you idiot," I continued, but aah was the only sound that left my sore cheek., I took a deep gulp of freshly polluted air then got off the bus.

"Good morning Mr Crawley," one of my students greeted.

"Good morning Luke," I replied, annoyed to be back, but happy at the same time. I walked through the school gates towards my classroom. I was greeted with many more repetitive good mornings. I stopped saying it with my lips, sinking to nodding as a lower form of salute and I covertly composed myself as I entered my classroom.

I made several steps through the door and was greeted by the smell of grubby teenagers, loud and excited, fresh from their weekend adventures. "Settle down, settle down," I shouted for attention. I began my lesson on the art of Shakespeare, babbling on like the beating of a drum to the ears of uninterested students, itching to escape my torturous words. *Shakespeare was a great user of words; my examination carried me, the kids in this classroom don't understand art.* The thought was interrupted by the striking of eleven o'clock; the lesson was over. They all left for their next lesson. I stood beside my desk with a glass of water in hand. What a terrible start to the morning, I reflected, my mind wondered to depths I did not know. For a little while longer I stood there, trying to take my mind away from the previous days, I hoped it...

Knock knock, the sound of my next class entering in a frenzy cut my reflection. Anticipating an earful of outdated words, they rushed in without consideration of silence, take a seat class. I cried out, hoping they would listen and follow the orders the first time, wishful thinking. I dreamed, echoing the same words, this time louder. The lesson began, this time with a smile on my face as time flew by.

"Hey James," a loud and girlish voice shouted, "how are you doing?" it repeated. It was one of the other teachers, I mentally noted, which brought my curiosity to a close; she had blurted the question out from across the hallway. It was strange, I thought, why didn't she just wait until she got closer. I wondered if she was too excited to see me. The students by this time were coming out for their lunch break; they rushed around like penguins in a ruckus, except it was less organised. I raised my hand to signal for her to come closer - I wasn't prepared to do as she did - I didn't want to shout my answers for others to scrutinise.

"I'm fine, thank you Liza," I exhausted, "thanks for checking on me, I'm doing a lot better," I further empathised, putting an end to where the conversation might have led. "The episodes are less frequent and I've had a break from the voice." I don't know why I felt comfortable telling her this, I don't know why it felt so free, but the noise in the corridor dulled so I was able to hear without arrowing my ears in her direction. She had a confused and puzzled look on her face as if she wasn't asking what I had just answered; the look in her eyes seemed distant, as if she was taking a step back in an attempt for her safety. I quickly changed the subject as we walked along the dated hallway and into the teachers' room, the smell of damp wood filing my nostrils. No matter how many times I walked through the school quarters, the smell remained the same. I discreetly flicked my nose to waver the bad smell away but it didn't work; of course it wouldn't. We walked in silence as if a sense of awkwardness was sprayed in the air. Liza comforted me when she placed a hand on my back, and rubbed it, something only Nicole was able to do. The silence broke when she suggested professional help, something I always hated, and still do. I did my best to angle my eyes in a way, that seemed thankful for her kind words. I was thankful but I just wanted her to shut up and leave me alone, I didn't want to tell her anything else, she's too nosey, I concluded. Well, that's what all the other teachers have said: within minutes of this conversation, the whole school would know. I didn't want to take that risk, the few words that slipped out were to be the last. I entertained her for a little while longer, until she slowly walked off.

"Hey Liza," another teacher walking by said, "what's all that about?" he faintly asked, but the sound wasn't low enough to evade my ears. I stayed quiet as if it did. Her gaze at him was too long, I wondered, it made me think that she had whispered something, something like, "I'll tell you later" and it only made me more paranoid and proved the theory of her deceitful tongue.

The final lesson was over as a sense of survival hugged me. I was happy it was over to say the least – *It's time to get out of here*, I said with the biggest grin on my face, *I mean, at one stage I loved being here, I loved the kids, the teachers, the atmosphere, but since lately, it's not been the same.* My shoulders were tight and it was a good thing I had brought my gym wear. "See you tomorrow Lisa," I waved. My footsteps sped down the rusty stairs to the exit of the school, the old creaky doors slammed shut as I pushed them a little too hard, and adjusting my backpack I motored on towards the bus stop. The sound of passing cars drew my attention, my wanting eyes stared as if to suggest the need for one, I quickly snapped out of it and produced a guilty smile.

The smell of freshly baked bread filled the air, making my stomach growl. All I had was a sandwich at the café, and that wasn't enough; the sound of children going home from school accompanied my journey; they bounced, played and shouted the previous episode of their favourite tv programme. It was nonstop. I hated this time of day to travel. Thinking back to the cars I saw earlier, wishing I had one right now, I wondered if the driver was the same from the last bus ride I took, I held on for my life that time. The bus took a turn so sharp it almost did a U-turn. *I think walking may be my new thing, or maybe cycling from now on*, I contemplated the idea, hoping not to be held accountable or charged for what I was thinking. "Stay away from the thought police," I murmured, giggling at a book I had previously read. I snapped out of the cloud I was floating on, the lazy in me said no; it's only thirty minutes' walk, I argued with myself, trying to find some logic in what I was saying.

A homeless man was sat on the floor, not too far from where I was. He seemed to be in his forties; slim build, sharp features, he didn't look dirty at all, and if he was to stand up and walk you would mistake him for someone going home from a hard day's work. I looked at him and thought he could do more, for the life of me I wanted him to do more, get out of the bubble, I screamed in my head, the system had him, I thought, breaking the connection of eyes from the windows of his soul, I pitied him. I didn't give him the coins I had swirling around in my pocket; he didn't deserve it. *Get up*, I summoned but he couldn't hear me as the thoughts kept rolling in.

"Get on that bus you fool!" a voice said. Frightened at the sudden intervention my body shook. "Not you again," I challenged, trying to put up a fight; I brandished my poker face to test whether he would back down and leave, but that didn't work as the voice continued to taunt and dominate me, "get on the bus," he continued. I was afraid; I wondered if he had done something to the bus. I know he was just a voice in my head, but he had more power than I thought - it was like he was sitting next to me with a gun to my head. It felt real. "I have a story to tell you," he continued in his monstrous tone. I didn't want any trouble, mostly because I was in public, but also because the day was going so well, and the bus was due to arrive in five minutes. I took a seat on the bench as I waited.

"Do you remember," he said, as if we were old friends catching up after years of absence. He continued, "when you was a child, how you loved your toys? You were almost inseparable from them, you was a happy child, filled with laughter and smiles. We used to play all day long, your energy was unmatched," he continued. At this point I was curious as to what he had to say, so I listened. "Your parents were the greatest, and they provided you with everything you could ever need, they 're every kid's dream." I looked back at the homeless man on the floor and suddenly felt warm; the moment was interrupted again as the voice asked, "you don't remember all of that, do you?" It sounded like he was telling me instead of asking, but he was right, I didn't remember. Silence filled my mouth as I had no response. "You was too young to acknowledge that you had a friend so close to you, someone that saw what you saw, felt what you felt, a friend." I interviewed myself; I don't remember a friend. I dug deeper. "It was me!" he shouted - not loud, but enough to ring my ears as his volume increased, "you was too young to care that you had someone like me, you stupid unimportant fool," the insult came from out of nowhere, "no one loved you like I did, no one is ever going to love you the way you were loved. You broke my heart," he said. His volume dropped and his tone softened, "but despite all that, I still thank you," his voice moved from the left ear to the right as if he was walking around a large empty room, except that room was my head.

The bus was running late. Five minutes had passed and the thought of the walk was becoming more appealing; it was like time had stood still. The voice was still in my head - I could feel him, I could hear his footsteps walking around even though the room was always empty, as if he was on a mission and wanted to be focused. A question slipped out my mouth faster than I could cover it. "Is that why you hate me, is that why you terrorise me? I was only five," I followed up, not giving him a chance to answer. I was reaching boiling point, my body becoming tensed and frustrated: "Why do I have to prove myself?" I asked. "I want an answer!" I demanded, "what do I have to do to get you to leave me alone or at least be nice?" I was now walking away from the bus stop, which had become filled with waiting passengers.

I didn't want them to hear the conversation, or should I say fight going on in my head and no sound left my mouth at that point. It must have looked strange from the outside; a woman with an overly large bottom was watching me: could she sense something, I wondered, or worse could she hear me? I continued to walk far enough to be away from them but not far enough to miss the bus. "Leave me alone!" I screamed, this time a sound echoing as it bounced off the shop window I was intently staring at. My reflection was somewhat strange; I looked different; I wasn't able to recognise my own eyes, I didn't like what I saw. *The battle is within*, I explained to myself, my breathing slowing as I realised my past has led its way to this moment. I needed to fix it - I still wasn't sure of all the details, but I needed to fix history in order to create a future, a future that involves peace. "I hate you," the voice intervened, "you can't get rid of me," he said. Strikingly, I was starting to believe him. "I am you and you are me," he educated, "we are one entity," he explained, "the only way I will no longer exist is if you die, no other way," he repeated, making sure I heard and understood. I stopped the breathing instantly as he uttered Nicole's name. It infuriated me and I clenched my fist, but control wasn't in my possession so I had to calm down. In the distance the bus was approaching. "Isn't she the love of your life?" he asked, taking advantage of my weakness, "my head has become your playground, a place where you feel you can do whatever you like." There was no response. I stepped on the bus, shakily, scanning for an empty seat. As the bus moved off, causing me to struggle for my balance, silence filled my head for a moment, as if we was taking a break to catch our breath. "All you want is to see me lonely," and with an evil tone the thunderous voice said, "YES! The unforgettable moment came that evening after you had your dinner. Unusually your parents were away from the fire place, leaving you to play as you normally did. They were in the kitchen this time, washing up, singing, laughing," his story continued as I gazed out of the window, my eyes narrowing in on the motion of the waving trees, thinking of the creation story I was told as a child. If there really was a God out there, why would he let this happen to me? My hand was on my head as the noise became too much to handle. "You killed your parents," the voice instantly yelled, a chill running down my spine as the weight of the words was like a dagger to the heart. "You threw your toys into the fire, I was there. You didn't listen as I tried to tell you not to do it. Your parents were in the kitchen as the fire spread, the fire alarm went off, they rushed out the kitchen to save you but the fire had already spread too far, the smoke in the air was thick and heavy, and sight was impossible. Your parents both fell as they tried to scurry out for clean air. The blanket they screamed to put over your head was enough to get you out; they coughed, screamed, cried, they were stuck, trapped and had no way out, but you left them to die," he alleged, as if he was twisting the already blooded dagger that was wedged in my back. It was painful to hear but I couldn't just close my ears - it was unstoppable. "For that, I will never forgive you," he ended. "I was scared," I cried out as I remembered my little legs carrying me out on to the front garden, "I didn't know - what to do, I didn't mean - to leave them in there," I spoke out, "I didn't know they were going to die," as I remembered the sirens blasting from the distance, "why didn't you tell me what to do?" I shot back at him, "why are you sounding holy," I fired again, "you was the one that told me to run, I remember, you was the one that said get out quick, don't you dare try put all this on me," I said in annoyance. I held back from swearing out loud. "Get away," I said with an ample amount of base and anger in my tone as I pressed the bell to get off the bus.

I pushed past the confused-looking passengers, bumping my knee on the pole at the exit, my groans of agony loud as I limped the rest of the way home. The feeling of who I once was kept replaying in my head even though the voice was gone now. I couldn't feel him no more but my body began to overheat like I was in the oven and I took a break from the pain in my leg by leaning against a wall that didn't look so stable. It was enough; an old lady walked past with two bags full of shopping and I looked at her with apprehension ignoring her with a slight roll of eyes as I continued to walk through the pain. Reaching my front door, I put my key in the door but I felt paranoid, so I turned around to see if someone had been following me. I barley turned round, with only a glance over my shoulders, then I opened the door and walked in.

CHAPTER 5

It was a Thursday morning with a new problem. Work was the last thing on my mind as I dialled the number. The lady that answered the phone gave a sense of, *not again*; her tone gave it away. "Depression," I said, and the voice on the other end changed instantly; it was warmer, more welcoming. "I need help," I said, depleting in my chair. She said nice things - how precious I am, and it gave a feeling like a hug through the phone; I felt it, and I hugged back. I couldn't believe this was the same lady I saw at work day in day out who never gave me as much as a good morning. It didn't matter - I needed the allies; she could go back to the same old Sue I see at work, it was ok, I uttered, but as long as I had her on the phone we were friends. The conversation went on for a further ten minutes, but nothing out of the ordinary was said, it was just generic questions. I answered, then hung up.

The wind blew and the sun peeped through the clouds, the cool breeze squandered its ways and freshened my body. A crack was now apparent in the mirror and my eyes connected with it. The reflection in the mirror was that of dark murky clouds, as if they were waiting to burst. In the mirror it looked like I wasn't in my living room, I was in a forest all alone, somewhere unknown to my memory surrounded by burnt trees. I instantly slammed my eyes shut and allowed my naked feet to carry me away while to wash away the dirt and fear that was laid bare on my irritated face.

The water ran hot as it slapped against my large frame, my head tilted up and looked into the heavens searching for the one they called father. The melted material pounded against my face as I looked up and I challenged it, my eyes hidden behind the lids covering them. Dreamlike, my right hand ran through my hair as the left held me steady, a vibration and a buzz distracting me as my moment of reflection was cut short. The text message was from Liza; she asked if I was ok - I suppose she had heard about my latest absence. I closed the phone and left it on the side, *unimportant*, I thought and got dressed. My phone buzzed again; annoyed I was ready to switch it off. A message from Robin, one of the few people in this world I liked. My mood changed; anytime I saw Rob I was always in a good mood - we have been best friends for a long time, going on thirteen years now and will be for a lot longer. I recalled when we first met, we were the only two fat kids in the class, our common weakness brought us together - we love windsurfing - and despite our size, we are pretty good. Why was he texting me? I wondered. Maybe to make sure I'm prepared for our trip next week. Opening the message, It read: "Meet me at the gym at 16:30." My reply was swift and short but filled with excitement.

The cab arrived late as it normally does and I was unimpressed. The driver knew what the expression meant. I seated myself at the back as I gazed out the window and I watched society go about their daily lives, my mind wondering if all those people were happy. I concluded *not, look at them*, I pondered, *probably on their way to a job they hate, rehearsing their line for the people they can't stand, practising their fake smile, correcting their tone of voice for fear of offending anyone, that's not happiness, how can we be happy at the regime and the fall in line status quo, they looked like lab rats, that could never be me,* I told myself, except it was, I was in the exact same position, I was caught up in the rat race. I paused, looking out the other side as if the perspective would be different. My mind was out of the system but my body was still in it, therefore I was trapped, I needed a way out. *If this is freedom, I don't want it: I remember when I was a child my thought was audible, unintended* - as the driver slightly checks on me as if I was talking to him, my childhood memories started to reel through the back of my eyes - *my parent's face was the first to run past, the worn out, dirty cab seat started to swallow me whole, my legs started to shake as if it was a jack hammer going through its foundation*, I rubbed and massaged my left arm and it soothed me, but I was still sad. *Her face was always soft, never looking her age, but the cracks in her forehead would make you question the generation she was from.* Unhappy memories were in full swing. "Was it really my fault"? I gazed at the bottom of my feet to see if the hole I had created was as deep as the abyss, but conveniently I was interrupted by the driver announcing the destination. The gym was just a short walk from the drop off, and it was enough time for me to forget the ordeal that was just playing in my head. Enough time for me to leave the question for the universe to answer: *was it really my fault?*

"Hey, Robin," noticing him standing by the entrance, the sound of my voice gave him a fright as he didn't see me coming. I laughed out loud, harder than I had laughed in a while, and he joined in seeing the funny side. I greeted him with a man hug, his large hand slapped against mine as it made a thunder clap and we walked in to the gym. The smell was still there. My eyes circled the place for managers - I wanted to make a complaint – but I settled that they were all hiding.

I was a couple strides behind Robin. I started to smile, almost breaking in to another fit of laughter. "Look at him," I thought, "5"6 tall and almost 5"0 wide." It was funny because I would constantly tease him about how short he was - he has an oversized stomach, thick brown thighs and chubby round face, he loves to make jokes and loves pranks. Our school days were filled with happy times and laughing is his favourite past time. It always bemused me why he didn't become a comedian; he has talent.

"Come on," he said, breaking up my thought, "we haven't got all day, get changed and let's hit the pads – it's boxing day today," he reminded.

"Are you my personal trainer now?" I asked sarcastically. He fired back with a sharp look, so sharp it made me think he was going to punch me. I got changed pretty quickly, and my warm up was swift, and rigorous.

Bang bang bang as my fist belts the floating bag, with a left and a right, *bang bang bang* as if I was letting out something, *bang bang bang* I skipped around getting in the groove, float like a what, sting like a what, I sung. Rob looked at me, his eyes suggesting I was crazy. He noticed the anger in each punch and he walked over to me: "Hey, are you OK? Why you hitting the pads so hard?" The question didn't hit my frontal lobe for a few seconds later. I tried to answer but I couldn't get my words out; my breath was running away from me and I had to chase it.

"It's been OK," I told him. With each word that came out, I had to pause. I realised only now that I was going too hard. I needed to leave some energy to walk and at least talk. I began telling him the situation that has been haunting me for a couple of days as I looked at him, still trying the catch my breath. I told him that I need help. "I've reached a stage where I'm becoming desperate, being amongst friends and keeping active is what I was told to try. I read it online."

I paused the words that were coming out, looked at him and he gazed back at me, and I could see in his eyes that he wanted to help me. He felt sorry for me, I could sense it. I took a seat on one of the machines nearby, slouching down as if I was a defeated boxer. I looked up at a standing Rob, and it further empathised my fate. In a slow soft tone I spoke of Nicole. It was always hard to speak of her without tears:

“I admire, cherish and adore her,” I told him as he stood in front of me with his ears pointed in my direction - exactly what I needed, and he knew that, “if anything was to happen to her, there would be no point of my existence; just her presence alone allows my foundation to be stable. I need her,” I cried out, looking in to his eyes as he into mine.

“Andreas,” Rob said, calling my name as if I was in trouble, “stop it, none of that is going to happen. Just concentrate on getting yourself back together. Everything will be OK, just take things one step at a time, control your emotions, be practical and realise your self-worth. Realise how important you are to a lot of people, stop being so fearful, come on,” he said as if he was giving me a half time talk. The gym was noisy so no one was able to hear his deep drum-like tone. “Connect with other people,” he added. “I know you don’t like to do that but you must, there maybe people that can help you.”

His advice was annoying but it sounded true; besides, he would never tell me something that he didn’t believe in. I nodded my head to accept the advice. “I can imagine what you’ve been going through,” he said, “but you won’t lose anyone else, and don’t let this son of a bitch control you. I’m always going to be here for you, my home is open for you,” as he stepped closer, “I will be your strength when you need it.” We wrapped up our session with cardio, and the conversation was left at that.

“See you later, Short Man,” I whispered, chuckling to myself as I walked off in the direction of home.

“Don’t forget out trip next week,” he shouted, ignoring my snide comment.

Hey,” Nicole said as she greeted me at the front door.

“I’m not doing too bad - I was at the gym today with Robin and it improved my mood.” I told her it calms the voice in my head and eases my anxiety, and I ended by telling her I’ll be doing it a lot more. She smiled at me and said she was happy, delighted that I am able to find a place of peace. She hugged me with her warm embrace; she smelled of daisy, her fingers were soft and delicate like the touch of a rose petal, her breath was warm and hypnotising. She stepped away from my arms and back into the kitchen. After five minutes of stirring she shouted: "Dinner will be ready in half an hour so get in the shower and take a seat." She said it with such affection in her tone. I did as I was told and got into the shower.

We sat at the kitchen table and watched as the birds entertained us through the window and my plate was clean within minutes.

"You worked up an appetite at the gym I can see." Nicole was always a slow eater. We spoke of wedding plans. "The dress," she said excitedly, "white or cream, with or without a Vail?" she asked. I had no clue of how to answer the question, so I told her I don't know, and she continued and said that she needed to go dress-shopping and that she would call her mother for help and hoped they could make some arrangements.

"Yeah, that sounds great," I responded, and she continued the happy spirit by teasing me, her eyes suggesting that she had a surprise for me. Anytime she was up to something she would have a glare in her eye, her pupils would become shiny and inviting. She looked at the bedroom, and gave me a suggestive look; it was strange but funny, so I gave her a smile. She looked sexy. I turned my head to look if there was any more food in the kitchen, I looked back at her and her dressing gown was half way off her shoulder exposing her red lingerie. She finished the tease by covering it out of sight, and she looked at me with a sexy seductive glance as her head tilted to one side. *I can see heaven in your eyes,* I thought, as I became uneasy with tension. I smiled with anticipation of what was to come.

The evening carried on in to the dark hours, and there was no sound or sight of the voice. I didn't want to think too much of him just in case he appeared and ruined the moment Nicole had created, all that layered my mind was to enjoy my soon-to-be wife, a moment that had been missing for a while.

With a glass of red wine in her hand she led me by the other; she placed a blindfold over my eyes. My anxiety started to boil up with deep breaths, I had to repeat to myself as she led me to the bedroom that smelt of scented candles. Through the blind fold I could see lights, purple lights that were shaped like stars, lavender. I inhaled again as she stood me in front of the bed, whispering in my ear with a soft breathy note, "don't move." The sound of clothing hitting the floor tickled my ears, *hers*, I thought, dressing gown from earlier. I smiled as she slowly removed the blindfold exposing her beautiful soft, silky, skin, her body shaped like a sculpture. I looked in delight, I scanned her up and down; her well-proportioned body was hugged by a red lingerie that exposed her erected nipples but covered her breast, the laced front was partnered by a thong that was attached to see-through stockings. She played with her hair and licked her lips as she gazed at me.

I wanted to touch her, but she slapped my hand and told me to watch. She danced for me, the kind of dance that would make a man give up his fortune; she brushed past me a few times, stroking my neck. I started to get hard; patience was running out. I wanted her, and I'm sure she could see the look in my eyes, the look of a predator getting ready to devour its prey, I held her by her hands and pulled her into my presence and we exchanged tongues. I ran my fingers down her body as her body moaned for more, the room was filled with ecstasy, the temperature turned to max as the windows were shut. I slowly stroked her from top to bottom, laying her on the edge of the bed, I licked her up and down as her body arched for pleasure. Her bra fell to the ground, then followed her knickers. Our bodies touched with an electric shock, sparking them to slide and rub; we felt each other's heartbeat. Our breathing synchronised; it increased as I entered her from the back and passionately and slowly we made love.

CHAPTER 6

The smell of sweet savoury mixture woke me from my sleep. I imagined it to be light and fluffy. *Nicole*, I thought. The room was still quite dark as my feet touched the floor, still buzzing from the night before. I traced my fingers across my chest like she had done. It was an airy morning filled with sunshine, cool and breezy, and revealing the curtains showed me the beauty that lay outside.

"Hey, what are you doing?" I asked curiously while approaching her as she moved around the kitchen.

"Making your favourite breakfast," she replied with a smile on her face. She smirked at my silly movements. I don't know what had come over me; it was her energy. She gave me life again, and this time I felt it was here to stay. My eyes caught hers before she could look away.

"Take a seat," she added. I took a seat near the window as we always do. The table was already set. A partition in the window halved and sectioned the table, allowing us to look through separate windows. I felt like a king and I could get used to it. My eyes continued to look out the window. The birds floated in a synchronised formation as they flew without care for the world. I imagined what it would be like to be free, I fantasied that it would be wonderful to be as light as a flock of feathers in the sky. I closed my eyes to allow the wind to beat against my face as I sat in my seat in a dreamlike state, wondering about the many mysteries that life has, wondering if I would ever be able to solve any.

I was strong enough to snap out of the dream and returned to reality. I peeked over at Nicole with the corner of my eye, and with my head tilted to the side, I fell back into the dreamlike posture, my thoughts travelling to the happy moments, the moments we created and shared together. The memories flicked one by one as I selected the day we met and I remembered how I felt the day I laid eyes on her. I remembered how she smelt, I took one final draw of air as my body went warm, I searched for her in the room, staring at her small frame, long legs, beautiful smile as she elegantly danced around the kitchen floor as if she was a gazelle manoeuvring around a field of obstacles. My mouth opened as I whispered my love for her. "I never want to lose you," I said with a touch of fright in my tone, a chill entering my space and removing the warmth that was once my comfort. The chill was the lingering voice that echoed in my empty skull; at the most quietest of times he would be there, as if he was watching me from round a corner, waiting for a moment to strike. He's like a stain of blood on the inside of a glass - you know it's there but you can't get rid of it, so you throw it away. I continued to ponder for a minute then snapped out before he appeared.

Her long black hair flowed down her shoulders as she took a seat in front of me she looked into my eyes with a loving, teasing smile. "Here you go my love. Did you enjoy last night?" The question caught me off guard. Taking a bite from the fluffy pancakes I proceeded to answer; only one word was needed. I replied, "SPECTACULAR." She giggled and continued to eat.

"We should go wedding-shopping today, we need to get things planned and in place before we find ourselves rushing around at the last minute."

"Yeah, that's fine," I responded with a reluctant look on my face. "You are right. We've only got a short while left until the wedding. We should go to that shopping centre you love so much."

She gave a soft smile before replying "yes, that's what I had in mind."

The bus ride into town was a quick one. It was bumpy and swerved with every turn. I'm starting to conclude that I don't like buses. I was seated by the window as I liked to look out into the world, not just to look at people but I wanted to see what was going on at all times. The shopping centre was rammed as we entered and they all seemed to be in a hurry. They moved like a herd of buffalos trying to find the nearest water hole; people pushed and bumped into each other. Did they care? I don't think so, they only had one thing on their minds; well, so it seemed, it was like they smelt blood once they laid eyes on a piece of garment they wanted - they knew no fear, for they only had one mission, and that was to buy. Who would have thought so many people would be hunting at the same time?

I looked around and remembered Rob's advice: give people a chance, he said. It was a hard thing for me to do, especially as I stepped out to what seemed like the playing field for animals, I gave them a chance nonetheless, but it was out of my comfort zone and I was out of my depth, the rash on my arm began to itch. It was becoming painful, but I continued anyway. "At what stage do they say enough is enough." Nicole turned and gave me a look to stop; she continued to looked at me like I was cramping her style. Was she listening? I don't know, but I was prepared to let her go off and do her own thing. I was prepared to sit by and wait.

"Don't these people have work?" She pretended not to hear, substituting a response with a swift change in direction.

Eventually we made our way to a few wedding shops – *Brides-To-be* it was called.

"Looking for a dress?" questioned the store assistant. I looked at her and had to hold my tongue with the sharpness of my teeth, like, why else would we be in here? I squandered for a reason in my head. Nicole, with more compassion than I, responded, "yes we are." The excitement and joy in her tone was apparent. She saw a dress in the window. "It's beautiful," she boasted. I agreed. "Wooow," she said in amazement as she expressed her warmth for an equally stunning dress, "that one looks really nice," she empathised as she turned to me for a matched expression; she didn't get it. The truth is I'm never excited about shopping - it usually takes too long - but Nicole, she was unable to contain her emotions. Her dances and twirls around the shops gave it away. "Let's go," she said as she hurried through the exit. "I just remembered that you are not allowed to see the dress." I gladly followed her out.

"You should be doing this with your sister or mother." She gave me a look of approval as we strolled through the shopping centre.

"Andreas," although she was right next to me; she shouted. I had no clue why but she shouted anyway.

"What is it?" I responded

"Come here, come quickly," she rushed as she continued to command my footsteps with her excitement, "what do you think?" she repeated continuously as her smile got larger.

"I think it's OK. I mean, I prefer the other one from earlier, it had a bit more elegance to it, but the one you walk down the aisle with will be perfect." By this time the smile turned from a frown and back to a smile again.

We grabbed a quick bite to eat and headed home. "Now I know exactly what I need to get," said Nicole, my body drained from all the walking I sat deep in the seat and promised myself shopping like this would never happen again, "now I know where to go and how much I need to spend," she continued bouncing around the bus like an excited puppy. How has she still got energy I wondered? My phone rang as the driver sped through the heavy traffic.

It was Rob calling. I picked up. "Hey Rob." At this point my heart had slowed down to the speed of Rob's tone; it was relaxed, steady and easy and the conversation was brief and to the point. It ended as I told him I would meet him at nine. Nicole turned her large eyes to me with a question on her face, waiting for an answer. Knowing the look, I smiled and said, "that was Robin; he wants to meet up later for a drink. He said he was treating me and I must come and have some fun." She smiled in acceptance of the answer. "It can only be a good thing, you go and have fun," she ended.

The clock on the wall read past eight o'clock. It was time for me to leave the house. Dressed in black jeans cut from the straightest of cloths, the slickest of brown shoes, a white shirt whiter than the whitest of teeth matched with a smart brown blazer, I was dressed to kill and smelling fresh. I was out to have a good night. "I will see you later," I shouted across the hallway, the notes reaching her ears as she ran to my location, gave me a kiss and told me to have a good time. "Be safe," she added. The taxi was downstairs waiting, and one last check in the mirror told me I was a ten out of ten. I entered the taxi and it took me to my destination.

Rob was standing outside waiting, yet again. I got out the car as if I was exiting a limo on to the red carpet of a movie premier. I looked at the car and gave the driver the seal of approval to leave. The other nod of approval came from Rob. He finished my entrance with praises only an A-List celebrity could demand and the energy rose to the roof as we embraced in a brotherly hug. The music was clear even from where we stood. We proceeded into the bar chatting and laughing. I felt as free as the birds in the sky from earlier that day. We moved with swagger and in the process bumped into a guy leaving for a smoke break - the bump was not hard but it was noticeable, it was like he had done it deliberately. I quickly turned and apologised to the unknown stranger. The strange looking figure, possibly drunk, staggered on to the outside, flinging his hands left and right as he tried to maintain his balance.

"Did you see that, Rob?" I expressed helplessly as I continued to walk behind. "No" Rob shouted with a perplexed look on his face, then shaking his head to empathize his answer. The host for the evening asked for the tickets, which Rob had. I was still confused and sure someone had bumped me. I looked back again to examine the contact with the stranger; I was sure it happened. My eyes penetrated through the long queue behind me, looking for an explanation, confused. I put the ordeal to the back of my mind and continued into the bar.

The mood was elated, vibrant and lively. We felt it and started to move to the music as our steps carried us onto the dance floor. We continued to side step our way through the crowd towards the bar to order some drinks.

"Can we get two beers, please?" Rob tried his best to shout his request through the loud thump of the base. We sat on a stool and waited, and then with a drink in one hand and the other clicking to the beat we moved back onto the dance floor. I looked at Rob and joked, "these people are not ready for our moves: we need to copy write them as quickly as possible," I continued to shout as if he was deaf, and we both laughed hysterically as we knew our dance moves were crap. We were in the mood to let loose. Our feet started to connect with the music. They made sense and I continued to dance without a care of what people thought of my two left feet, the alcohol flowed side by side with my blood causing a numbness to all senses of judgement. By this stage we'd had quite a few. I was enjoying myself; for the first time in a long while I had been out enjoying the sound of music and my hate for people disappeared with my fear. Rob was right - as I began to enjoy the floor with others, giving out high fives and laughing like we were long-time friends.

It was a good night. I cared not about anything as I was interrupted by an infamous tone: "What are you doing here boy?" the voice shouted down my ear, patronising and belittling. Turning around expecting to see someone I knew, I found no one, no one that I knew, no one that would say those words, only dancers enjoying the music. *Who said that,* I thought. Intoxicated, I continued to dance, thinking I was drunk and hearing things, I don't know why I thought that but I did, as I closed my eyes in disbelief and fright, anger filling my eyes as I clenched my fist to the point of drawing blood. I opened my eyes and released the clench, only to find red blood stained marks on my shirt. The voice repeated, "what are you doing here?" This time the tone haunted me and I readied myself for a fight. Rob was about two feet away from me, unaware of what was happening, but the fight was about to begin. I grabbed my head again, this time going down to my knees I pleaded with the voice, "pleasssssssse leave me alone." I shouted it again, this time in a trembling tone as tears filled my eyes while the music continued to pumped, the base rumbling over the agony I was facing.

Rob noticed what was happening and rushed to my side. "Andreas!" he shouted, "what's happening?" he asked, demanding an answer, panic in his voice. I looked up to a worried looking set of eyes. "What can I do to help?" he yelled. The music was not backing down as the voice continued to taunt me, "you stupid useless fool," his voice deepened like it was coming from a valley, "do you think you can get rid of me by being with your friend?" his voice now sounding sickened at the thought, "having fun," he continued, "getting drunk," he ended, "do you think I am that stupid, do you take me for a fool? You will suffer for as long I say you should, maybe it should start with your friend Rob, maybe he should suffer like you."

His words cut me deep as I searched the labyrinth of my head for a way out. "That will be a long time," he laughed, an evil long lasting laugh that dragged on for a while. "I need him to leave me alone," I shouted and tears filled the spot I was stuck to. "I want him to just die," I bawled out as I rocked back and forth to sooth the pain, to ease the noose from my neck. This time the scream was over the music and people on the dance floor started to look and stare. They whispered to themselves. The music was still pumping as the DJ noticed that no one was moving to his brilliant selection and noticed a commotion.

He pressed *pause* on the track as the place fell into dead silence. My ears rung as I got up from the floor. I staggered to my feet, going down once more as my knees felt weak. Rob held me as I walked outside. We bumped into people and stepped on a few toes, knocking drinks over as we made it outside without going down again. Outside was dark and cloudy; it was like the summer had ran away from where I was, *probably scared of the voice*, I thought. The sky showed no stars, they too were afraid; the light from my life was diminishing and it was hard to see fifty meters down the road. The pavements were covered with pixilated blackness. "There he is!" I shouted, "that was the guy that bumped into me as I was coming in, he is the one in my head, he caused this!" Becoming more and more agitated I found the energy to burst away from Rob and headed straight for the unknown guy. He was dark - I was never able to make out his face, it looked like he didn't have any facial features, just a shape of a person. I headed for thin air; punched and connected with a lamp post, hoping the punch would connect with the voice's face. no one was there, it was all in my head. I was the only one able to see this guy or should I say figure. I wanted to hurt him; my anger was spilling over like an over-filled drum of oil. I continued to argue with the unknown, asking why. I followed the wind into the cloudy distance but Rob rushed to me once more and grabbed me before I was able cause any more damage to myself, or anyone else for that matter.

"I will contact my wife's friend," Rob murmured. "I will ask him to make some room for you - you need professional help," he ended.

CHAPTER 7

A couple of weeks had passed, and the voice was in and out of my head. With every happy moment, there he was. Darkness followed me; it was him: outside was no longer appealing. I had no desire to shower or even entertain my loved ones; he kept reminding me that he will never leave me. His words became my reality; I believed him - I had no hope. I sat in my gloomy house, waiting to evaporate and be forgotten.

Nicole walked around the house. I barely noticed her. Her flow was different, and her gaze was judgmental. The beast in my head had blurred everything I knew. Rob told her what happened at the club. I heard his basely voice on the phone. Her face was terrified. She broke down halfway through and looked at me. She just stared without saying a word; she didn't have to say anything. I already knew.

The scented candles had vanished and left a smell of dead flesh. The whiff bounced from wall to wall without a route of escape. I checked my hand to see if I was rotting away, but I was ok for now, at least. I gazed out the window in search of the birds. Daydreaming became my safe place, a place where I could go and be away from this world, from my problems. It was a place where I couldn't be touched, I had no responsibilities there, and I had created my reality. I loved it there!

There was always a voice on the outside trying to penetrate inwards; Nicole was that voice. She constantly called my name in search of me. It was like I was lost to her, lost in a field of hay. The wind came crashing into the living room and blew a cup from the counter, breaking it with a smash. Pieces of glass scattered and flew everywhere. We both jumped in fright then looked at each other before she attended the crime scene.

"That scared the hell out of me," I said in anger.

I paced over to the window in a fury and slammed it shut. Nicole rushed out of the room headed straight for the toilet, and I went straight after her. I was confused. Had she cut herself and seen blood? I wasn't sure. She hated the sight of blood, so it was possible.

"What's the matter?" I called out to her. She didn't reply; how could she? After all, her mouth was filled with vile liquid.

The volume of liquid flowing made it difficult to control. It splashed all over her hair and face. She lifted her head in disgust and turned to the sink. I stood there watching her. She was helpless, and so was I. A sudden urge told me to hold her hair back. I wasn't much of a helper, so I was slow to the call. She finished emptying her stomach, rose to her feet, and washed her mouth from the little bits stuck under her tongue. She finally got the chance to answer my question.

"I'm late," she said.

I narrowed my eyes as if I was looking through fog.

"What are you talking about?" I asked, still perplexed. I repeated her statement, followed by "late for what?"

"I missed my period last week," she explained, "I haven't done a test but it seems I may be pregnant."

My eyes lit up in delight, and I glowed like a Christmas tree while hugging her. I'm sure she felt the heat. An aroma from her breath travelled the depths of my nose, but it was bearable.

"You need to get a test," I told her. "In fact, I'm heading out to sort something out and I will get one." She nodded with a big grin on her face.

Still buzzing from the good news, I ran out of the house. My chunky legs took me down the flight of stairs quicker than they usually did. My neighbour was at the top of the stairs.

"Good morning." I shouted as I reached the bottom. Not knowing his name to add one to the greeting, "How are you doing?" I continued. He stood at the top of the stairs looking like a giant, a king standing over his servants. But in reality, up close, he was only about 5ft 2—full head of white hair like a polo bear from the north with brown wrinkled, leathery skin.

Whenever I see this old man, a robe can always be found flung over his shoulders. He always has a bead around his wrist. Sometimes he plays with them. I'm curious as to what they are, but I'm too timorous to ask him. I shook my head. A mystery encircled him, a strange feeling. I can't quite put my finger on it. He lives on his own because I never see anyone else go in or come out in all these years. He was here when we moved in, and never had a problem with him since. He always has an invitation for me into his place.

"Some of my special tea," he would say in an accent unfamiliar to my knowledge, I have never made the time for him.

He seemed to love interacting with people, a very nice person, I must say. One day, I thought we would have the time and sit down to share some wisdom with me. His one-eyed dog strolled out from his side. He lazily moved as he rocked from side to side. He was a chocolate Labrador with grey spots along his nose. His mouth was soaking wet like he had just finished his morning coffee. He looked as old as the old man did with droopy eyes.

"Surely his time is soon," I thought. The one eyed dog stared at me as if he was telling me to go away. He gave me the feeling that I had overstayed my presence. I read the message loud and clear, and I said my farewell. I reached the car I had rented for the day, "maybe longer," I thought, depending on how it goes.

The car drove well. It was better than waiting at a bus stop only to be cramped up like in a sardine tin. I'd grown fed up of that. It was only minutes after leaving when my phone started ringing. It was Nicole. I thought she was throwing up again, so I picked up as quickly as I could, only to be met by a screaming police car. His eyes caught mine with a sinister look.

He shook his head slowly to suggest, "I wouldn't do that if I was you," then carried on without stopping.

"Are you ok?" I asked as I rung her back.

"Yes," she said as normal as ever, "where are you going?" she asked.

Something in my mouth had a hold of my tongue. It took me five seconds at least to answer.

"I'm going to visit the house my parents died in."

I could hear the air leaving her body as I mentioned it. I'm sure it must have felt like a heavy weight boxer had winded her. She asked why and I quickly told her I needed to close a chapter, I needed to see if I could feel something.

'Anything," I added.

I hung up the phone as she was satisfied with my determination.

Arriving at the house, I waited out of sight though not so far that I couldn't see the front door. It seemed as if someone was expecting me; there were spaces to park. That was never the case in a place like London. The property was burnt to ashes. Everything was blackened and left exposed. Though I had never seen it with my own eyes, I'd imagined it was so.

But now it was a newly built palace, and it looked beautiful. I noticed the reddened bricks neatly packed at the front, then flowing round to the side of the building; it had three bay windows. Each window went up and up, one by one, suggesting there were three floors. The door was sea-foam green. It had a wall tree growing along the walkway just above the archway of the door.

I was taken aback as I sat in the car, admiring from afar. I never dared step out of the car to go any closer.

"Was it haunted?" I thought.

I shuffled in my seat as it got uncomfortable. The front garden was filled with flowers and greenery. It reminded me of the times my father would bring my mother velvet roses, her favourite, I thought. She used to take long whiffs of them each time she entered the room. I stepped out of the car defying my earlier thought. I needed to get closer. I needed to feel the energy left for me.

I looked at the front door and remembered the many times I ran in and out playfully. I tripped and fell most times, but I was being chased by dad. Dad came out of my mouth again. It felt weird, like there was no attachment to it. No meaning, feeling or accountability, It was just a word that floated in the atmosphere, waiting to connect with something tangible.

I took a couple more steps closer to the gate. Wary of looking like a thief, I stopped short of the gate. Tears filled my eyes. It was a common thing for me to be crying. I was pleasantly surprised that I had no tears left. I went back to the car, this time standing outside leaning on the bonnet.

"I knew you would come back, the voice said. He would always appear at times where I was uplifted, tranquil and felt a sense of progression.

I cursed under my breath as I walked from the front of the car to the back.

"Welcome back, Andreas," he prolonged, "you have been missed." His tongue hissed like a snake, and it was fitting considering his slipperiness.

I didn't react how I would have a couple of weeks ago, and I knew by now how this story goes so I played along as best as I could. I stepped into the car, looked in the mirror, and shouted at the top of my voice.

"Yes, I have returned! there was no way I could avoid this place for much longer. You dug up something that was buried a long time ago, so I had to come back." my voice slowly came down to normal levels.

"Tell me something," my voice was now faint as if I was whispering. I didn't know why I went that low, but I did. "What's your motive?" I continued, "why are you here?"

"First of all, I was your best friend," the voice answered as it gladly took over "now, I am your worst enemy, the side you feed the most becomes strongest. This house is where we lived. It was my sanctuary, we was loved by our parents, cherished, adored. They were great parents. I never wanted any of this to happen." he continued in a calm tone. It was like he was hurting as well, like he had lost just as much as I did. It didn't make sense. He seemed gentler while he was speaking. There was no sign of any insults coming from his way of speaking. His mind was clear and focused. It was like this location brought peace to him. "It was all your fault he ended," Mr nice guy had changed back to the devil.

That lasted long, I thought.

"You started the fire!" he irked.

The sun was blazing down on the car I was in, so I cracked the window for air. This particular day was one of the hottest of the year so far. The voice continued to babble on, and the sound moved from corner to corner of my head. It was like he was walking around with his hands interlaced behind his back. Like you normally see in movies of interrogation.

"I became like this after we went to foster care," he continued, "Bridge Town Care it was called," he recollected with ease. "The abuse that I endured was unbearable. No food for days, unwashed clothes often bared the scent of urine, faeces-- they said we needed to be punished. We didn't get anything except the opportunity to draw the short straw from the palm of life's hand. No water, not to mention the sexual abuse; they each took turns. It only lasted about two minutes or so, but it felt like an eternity—the smell of sweat stained my nose and I despised the smell ever since. There was blood the first time it happened. I screamed in agony. The sound of the zipper going up and the button of his pants locking was what gave me hope of survival, I appreciated it and each time I thanked him for stopping.

My eyes started to flow once again as the images of the story came back to me. I could feel it all over again.

"Why did you remind me of that?" I asked him. "why?" I shouted in pain.

He didn't answer. The empty room in my head was silent. The voice said nothing.

"They must pay," I thought.

"That's it," uttered the voice, repeating it, this time with a smirk on his face. "That's it, that's exactly what I wanted to hear because it is necessary. These people need to pay. We had to be tough to survive the ordeal," he continued to recall. It was like he was clenching his fist, rallying the troops, his one-man army.

"It wasn't a nice place," he added, "certainly not a place for a 5-year-old. It brought the worst out of me," he noted. "It created a monster in me. You see Andreas," (I hated when he called my name), "I'm out to hurt those who damaged us. I had to be tough for the both of us, I developed a sense of hatred. I wanted revenge for all those that hurt us. All the carers, everyone that knew what was going on and done nothing. Everyone that stood back and laughed, while they went home to their families driving their nice cars and eating good food. I hated life. There was nothing to love at that time. I contemplated jumping down the rabbit hole, disappearing and never to return but you were in my way. You held me back, you didn't want to listen, you was soft," he raised his voice at me, ringing my eardrums.

"You never carried out any of my commands. I told you to sneak away and call the police, tell them everything that was happening, tell the support workers that weren't involved. You was in control at that time. I was only a little voice in the back of your head, no power, no strength. How things have changed," he spoke in a slow purposeful tone. "I will get the revenge I have longed for."

I interrupted as my body started to shake, the sun was shining, but my feet were freezing. Pedestrians walked by as they noticed my stature shaking. They must have assumed I was on drugs because they carried on walking.

"He looks unwell," a lady's voice said on the way past. I took my head out of my hands. My left arm was itching again, and my fingers felt like a saw blade as it drew against my arm.

"What do you want me to do?" I asked reluctantly.

"I want revenge on the people that hurt me," he said quickly and happily, "I need you to kill them."

I widened my eyes in disbelief. "Did I hear right?" I asked.

"Yes," he said. I looked around to see if anyone had heard the outlandish request until I remembered it was all in my head.

"This is not something I am capable of," I replied.

"There are three of them I want you to eliminate," he demanded, ignoring my last plea of pardon. "Then you will be free from me. I will be gone from your life; the power will be yours. If you do not do this, I will cause you to harm everyone you love. First your friend, then your fiancé with a child on the way," he said with an evil laugh.

The conversation was done, and the voice disappeared like a magician. I started the car and left the scene. Everything was playing on my mind,

"It was my fault; it was all my fault. I have to accept the consequences of my actions and move forward to make things better."

The deal that was agreed with the demon was my next challenge. I needed to do it, or my loved ones were going to suffer by my hands. I needed a bulletproof plan.

"I'm not made for jail," I thought. Everything needed to be an accident, whether they slipped and fell or a car hit them down.

"It can't tie to me," my mind was now overpowered with thoughts of murder.

Whether it was justified or not, it was still murder. The idea was haunting me, and my mind crept over to Nicole.

"I must protect my family," I vowed.

My mind continued to drift in and out of reality as the car steadily took me down a long stretch of road. BONG! was the sound from the front of the car, Either the engine had blown up, or a tyre had blown out. I swerved the car left and right, almost losing control. I heard the sound of cracking against the front bumper. I checked the dashboard; there were no lights, the car felt the same. I stopped by the side of the road only to find blood splattered all over the car's front. I looked back down the road, and a fox laid on the ground. Its body laid in the middle of the road, flat, tongue out, eyes rolled back, and legs rearranged into a puzzle. Instantly the voice appeared once more and said,

"Just like that, well done."

I continued without looking back in the rear-view mirror.

Car wash, I thought.

I reached home and entered the key in the door, the old man's door made sounds as if he was coming out. Our eyes connected; the old man looked through me. It was like he could see everything, like he knew me, who I really am.

"Are you OK, young man?" he asked. "Compared to how I saw you earlier you don't look so well."

"I'm OK," I replied while continuing through my door to avoid any more questions. The old man scared me. Not like the voice did, but he scared me like a best friend would finish your sentences.

"Hey honey," Nicole rejoiced, "how was your day? How was the visit?"

I kicked my shoes off and replied,

"it was ok, it wasn't as bad as I thought it would have been." Knowing I was lying, I turned my head in shame, unable to reveal all the details to her. She can never know I trembled.

"Well, I had a good day, thanks for asking," she joked. "I did some wedding shopping and planning," she continued to beam, "I also got tired of waiting on you for the pregnancy test so I got it myself and took the test."

My face lit up again momentarily, like how it was before I first stepped out.

She continued,

"We are having a baby," her voice escalated from start to finish.

She giggled with excitement, and my face shone brighter than the stars that evaded the sky that night. I hugged her to accept the news.

"Are you hungry?" she asked.

"No thanks," I replied sharply.

I noticed the covered mirror in the living room. A little piece was exposed, showing my left eye. I stared at it for a while before adjusting the position to cover it fully. I thought back to when the voice mentioned Nicole having a baby. He knew before I did,

"How is that possible?" I wondered, but of course, I didn't get a reply.

It got dark pretty quickly, and the mood matched the exterior of the house. The sky was dark with no stars present. The moon shone, waiting for the darkest of things to develop in the brightest of minds.

I stared out the window for a while, wondering what life would have been if my parents hadn't died, I snapped out of the fantasy and closing the curtains.

That night I went to bed restless as usual, but this time it was not like any other nights. I had a terrible dream. The fox that I hit earlier followed me back to my home and was now in my bed. Nicole was not there. She was gone.

"Where?" I thought.

The dream continued, I got out of bed to investigate. The fox laid in her spot. Its tongue was out, and its eyes rolled over, looking at me. They followed me as I moved around the room, his legs rearranged but still breathing.

I woke up in a panic that morning, wondering if it was real, Nicole was there next to me. She was still sleeping. I sluggishly got out of bed before the sun had risen. It was a grey Saturday morning and the newscaster was reporting another terrorist attack, twenty-five dead in an explosion near the city Centre of Paris, France. The house I visited yesterday was strange, I couldn't explain it, but the feeling was mysterious. I needed to find out more.

CHAPTER 8

The sun crept its way up to its destination as it brought me into the spotlight. My face lit up like a lone star missing from the sky. The birds from the other day were back. This time they sang a good morning melody. My eyes carried my feet to the window. It was bright, so bright my eyes narrowed to focus on a single object. I had to pinch myself to see if I was still dreaming.

I wasn't so lucky. The plan rang in my skull like the echo of a bell after it has been struck. The air outside tasted as bitter as grapefruit maybe and the smell of it caused my nose to itch.

"Time to meet our old enemy," the voice said cheerfully.

"You're up early," I shot back. It wasn't a friendly fire. It was aimed at his head, I missed. I spun around and away from the window as my morning gaze was interrupted by Nicole. She came strutting into the kitchen as if she was on a runway of a fashion event, her hair out and it blew with the wind.

"I must protect them both," I faintly said to myself as I watched her move.

"Get moving," the stain in my head said, cutting my thought short.

I felt like I was at gun point; my choices were to kill or be killed. I began to plan the crime. Nicole was on her way out and running late for work. In all the rush, she never forgot about me. She wore a short black skirt, exposing her long soft legs. I watched them as they came closer until she was in my face. She grabbed the tip of my chin and guided it up to her delicious red lips. She gave me a kiss that almost said I love you, without the words passing them. The voice reminded me today would be the last I got to kiss her in such way.

I searched the internet for the old employees. The search didn't take long; everyone's on social media nowadays. All their information is plastered, just waiting for someone like me to find them. I quickly found a list of names, as the voice spotted the ones that caused the damage.

"Jimmy the security guard," he whispered in my ears, "Sara the carer and Edith the manager." He smiled at progress, knowing he was getting closer to what he wanted. I felt a chill down my spine.

"I'm scared," I said faintly, hoping Nicole would hear me wherever she was.

I was nervous at the thought of carrying out this act of violence.

"This isn't me. Although I despise this society and all the sheep's in it, I never wanted to hurt anyone. It's too late," I thought.

He wasn't going to let me off. I felt myself changing, and my skin grew tougher. I stopped recognising myself. I was now him.

"Get up and stop feeling sorry for yourself," a stern voice cut through my sorrow like a knife through butter. "We have work to do, that pretty lady will not come back tonight if you are not careful."

The tension in the room became radioactive, waiting to explode. I was ready to smash up the whole place in the hope of destruction, but I couldn't.

"You need to be on the dark side, he continued," he was enjoying this. I could feel him.

"You need to have the balls to do this because if you get caught, you are the one going to feel it," he shouted, unleashing spit with every word.

I wiped my face as my finger moved on the keyboard like a formula one car in hot pursuit of victory. I searched for the address using a little trick Rob taught me, and within minutes, I had found them. My heart blackened as I realised the voice meant business and was not to be taken lightly.

The window became my sanctuary, a glimmer of hope. It allowed me to see far beyond my troubles. I was free while my mind was outside the four corners—something to grab on to or at least touch with my fingertips. My sanity floated alongside the birds, and it became the only way to separate myself from the reality created for me. The dark side appealed to me. Maybe this was me all along. Or perhaps it was created by my circumstances. Either way, I was about to taste blood.

"Stop it," the voice intervened, "we belong together, joining forces and working together at long last, this is a natural phenomenon."

I rolled my eyes in annoyance, annoyed because the fact was true. We were one, and it was like that for a long time.

"What's the plan?" he asked.

I was still seated around the table as my gaze broke from the outside world. I turned my head to answer him. I looked at the chair in front of me as if he was seated there, directed all my energy to him, and said,

"The plan is to go after the manager first."

I remember her face, her laughs. She seemed to enjoy it the most. She led the ordeal. She organized it.

"See you same time next week," she would say. She deserved to die first.

It was like I smelt her blood. At the moment I was Dracula, I licked my lips.

"I have her address; she lives with her husband. He usually goes away on business, couple days at the least."

"Go on," my new ally said.

"I will break into her house, knock her out, tie her to a chair and then question her. Yes, question her," I repeated. "I want to know why she did what she did." I slammed my fist on the table, alerting a cup to jump and fall to the ground.

Thinking about what she did, angered me.

"I want her to know who I am before," I paused, "before I strangled her. It's a simple plan," I sounded out.

I looked up, searching for his eyes. I found none, so I closed my eyes, and there he was. His pale white face smiled at the idea, and his lips made way, exposing his pearly white sharp teeth.

The afternoon fast approached. I heard the door knock, causing me to jump out of my skin.

"They know the plan," I thought.

My mind travelled to the horrible breakdown I had.

"Are they still peeping through the key hole?" I wondered.

I walked over; as quiet as a mouse searching for food. I opened the door gingerly, and to my relief, it is my neighbour, the old man.

"How are you doing?" he said. His tone sounded worried. He continued, "I heard noises from your place earlier. I thought I should check if everything was ok."

I smiled at the kind concern.

"You're not being held hostage," he asked with a smirk on his face.

I laughed out loud as if it was a joke. It wasn't physical or anything anyone could see, but the joke was real. I was being held, hostage.

"No, everything is fine." I replied unconvincingly.

He looked past me as if he didn't believe me. If only he could see what was beyond my eyes, he would have noticed the shadow lurking in the background.

"I was talking to myself," I added, bringing his concerns to ease.

"Ahhhh'" the old man responded, "something I know all too well," he said as he walked off, wishing me a good day.

Nicole wasn't due back until later; she was at a friend's house. I got myself ready to leave. The numbers on the clock read 22;00. it was a Sunday, and the road was empty. It was only entertained by the usual suspects: prostitutes and drug dealers. A few cars filled the lanes but nothing uncommon. The air tasted like off milk, thick and vile. Like something was in the air.

I cruised to my destination as if I was enjoying a night stroll. I watched all the lights on the streets like it was a Hollywood scene. I wondered if this would be my last moment of freedom or whether this will be the beginning of the end.

Before the idea of peace was able to take shape in my head fully, the memory of the dead fox entered the frame. I should have said cut right there, but I couldn't. The movie went on; it stained my eyelids, almost blinding me to the fact that death is a one-way road. I had no brakes, and there was no turning back now.

Once again, it felt like a parking space was reserved for me. Before I pulled up, I had to double-check that I had all I needed.

"Mask -check, cable ties-check, and the rope I will to use to strangle her- check."

My palm was no longer sweaty, but I could smell the sweat patches under my arms. Nerves took hold of me while I looked through her curtain-less window. Her face was hidden with her back turned. I watched her move freely as if she was practicing some kind of dance. She flowed like an innocent person as if she knew what was to come. I was her maker, and she was about to meet me.

The cool evening breeze blew, which attracted dog walkers. I had to be careful. I slid down, hiding my suspiciously large figure in the car. I made no sound as the elderly man walked past; I was safe.

I waited until the lights in the house had gone off,

Now's the time, I thought.

I excitedly ran out of the car without locking it behind me. I wore black gloves just like in the movies, with a hood over my head slightly covering my face. The knock on the door was subtle, but it was enough to alert anyone inside. I prayed she didn't turn the lights back on. If she had, I would have been doomed, but she didn't. She opened the door slightly to check who it was.

"It's too late," I shouted, in my head, of course. The adrenalin was pumping. By the time she noticed it was an uninvited guest, I was through the door. I bagged her head and used the other hand to cover her shouts for help.

"It's all happening," I thought as she bit my finger in an attempt to escape my strong grip. Her body trembled against mine; she looked like she feared for her life. While her words under the tape were,

"Please don't rape me. Please."

I was silent and still said nothing. Raping her was never my intention; she had every right to fear what I was to do to her just like I did while she took my innocence. I didn't show her any mercy. I pushed her into an empty chair knocking her head against the wall. I tied her legs and hands behind her back. She squirmed, trying to hold on to the last glimmer of hope left in her inner strength. She started to panic, letting off a few more screams. It fell on deaf ears as the sound didn't penetrate the lock on her lips.

"Do you know why I am here?" I finally spoke, "do you know who I am?". I continued raising my voice, slightly causing it to go higher.

Her demeanour was more relaxed as she heard my voice. Maybe she thought it was a soft voice, and she was to be safe because there was no way this soft voice was going to hurt her. Or maybe, it reminded her of a voice that used to read her bedtime stories. I didn't know which, but her shoulders dropped.

It was strange; she was no longer struggling to get free. Did she know who I was? I thought frantically. I shook my head in disbelief, dismissing that idea as ridiculous. She was becoming more audible, as if she was trying to communicate something to me.

The voice entered the party, and he was adamant she knew who I was.

"She knew this day would come," he said in a deep dark tone. His voice frightened me. It sounded like it bounced off trees in a dark forest.

"She doesn't want to die," he added, "why wouldn't she try to prolong things? get on with it!" he snapped.

"My name is Andreas," I spoke, "when I was five years old I was in a foster care home." I continued to remind her of what she and her friends did to me.

"I hated myself, I hated life and wanted to die every day I was there. why didn't you just put me out of my misery and kill me?" I shouted, now standing in her face.

"I would have thanked you in the afterlife for it, but here we are now. I hate you for what you did to me, and I will make all of you pay for what you have done."

I prepared myself to take her out, the rope tightly gripped in my hand, ready to take the breath from her body - but I wanted to look into her eyes; I wanted to see her soul through the windows of her eyes. I slowly began to remove the hood from her face, her body still relaxed. I was shocked at the sight of the face - it couldn't be possible, I said, stumbling back. I wanted to run out but the voice said: "stop" and so I did, "look her in her eyes" and so I did – I was now his puppet and he was my master; I couldn't break the trance I was in while my eyes fixed on her, and my cheeks felt sore like he had punched me. I looked at the face again: it was Nicole's sister, her eldest sister; the same sister that she no longer spoke to.

"This can't be, this must be some sick joke," I called out. "Where are you?" I cried out. "Did you know who she was?" I asked.

He didn't answer. I felt lost, hot, cold, and I didn't know what to do. I was just about to kill my fiancés sister.

"Fuck it, she done me wrong, no; I thought I could do this. How could I live with myself?" As much as Nicole hated her, she would still be devastated.

"What if I don't do it and she tells Nicole what I have been doing? My life would be over! I can't let this happen, I must kill her," I said as I put the hood back on her face. I didn't want her to look at me any longer.

Before I had finished the last word, the voice jumped in with a thunderous tone. I felt like I was at a festival as the bass rang my ears.

"Continue with the plan, you fool," he shouted. "I don't like to repeat myself and I will not remind you again what is at stake. She needs to die; she needs to pay for what she has done. One way or another someone will pay, let it be her and not you. Final warning my friend," he said furiously.

I sat down in the chair closest to me; it still felt warm.

"I've never seen Nicole's sister in person. I've only seen her in old pictures, and she didn't look like this. Oh my God! what am I going to do?" I went into panic mode again.

Nicole used to talk about how she never came to family functions, how she has distanced herself from the rest of the family, and with this thought it was as if a light bulb was switched on.

"Could this be the reason?" I took the hood from her head and the tape from her mouth.

"Do you know who I am?" I asked.

"Yes'" she replied, still terrified as if she thought what I was doing was fully unjust.

I circled her as silence filled the room; a pin could be heard darting its way to the floor as I released the grip of my fist. The tape went straight back on her mouth and her eyes were now closed in anticipation of the worst or maybe the best - just maybe she wanted to die. Perhaps it was the only way to rid her of the guilt, but did she even feel guilty? None of that mattered now.

"One down, two to go," I said, counting on my fingers.

She started to tremble again, this time bouncing her feet furiously as I whispered, "I'm sorry."

I took small strides to stand behind her and my hand rested on her shoulder, creeping its way to her neck. I threw the rope away; I wanted to feel the pulse in her neck disappear, I wanted to feel her go, and so my grip tightened around her neck as her feet began to kick in search of air. The chair made sounds of distress as she went to and fro in it and started to foam at the mouth as her kicks got shorter and softer. I released the grip before her eyes had rolled back, and she somehow managed to find the air that was missing a minute ago.

She coughed and coughed as her body rebooted. I walked round to the front so that I could see her face once more.

"Continue to remain a ghost and make sure to keep this our little secret," I whispered in her left ear while on my knees so I could see her and she could see me.

"If you ever make the mistake and say a word I will come for you and I won't stop until your tongue flops out. Do you understand me?" I asked, making sure she understood my command.

I cut her hands loose and slipped out the door I had entered. I ran to my car as I wasn't sure whether I could trust her, started the engine and left. I lost again; I was staring at the worst to come. I was back home with no blood on my hands, and only the couch comforted me as Nicole was fast asleep. The sheet that once covered the mirror in the living room had fallen to the ground exposing the truth, and I turned around and stared at myself. I looked shameful, guilty, and dead.

"Is this who you've become?" I asked quietly before leaving the house again, this time to end it.

CHAPTER 9

I woke up unaware of where I was until I bumped my head on what turned out to be the hand brake. Despite the instant pain that shocked my system, there was a knocking sound coming from somewhere. It sounded like it was coming from outside, but it was close. Furthermore, my head was pounding, and my eyes fogged. When a final thump came crashing against the window, I was alerted of the fact a ticket was issued to my car.

"Shit!" I shouted as I finally jumped out of my lazy state; as a consequence, the bottles on the floor clattered, and almost smashing.

I quickly adjusted myself, then wiped my eyes and scampered to get the car moved. Admittedly it's been four days since I had the car. Extending it wouldn't be wise. I checked my phone and noticed forty-five missed calls and 38 messages, all from Nicole and Rob.

She must have called him asking for my whereabouts, along with her worries for my mental health. Undoubtedly, my mind went to the voice. He hadn't been in my ear since the last warning was issued for this reason.

"I need to prepare for when he does return, clearly I need help," I thought.

The car rolled along the busy roads as I unquestionably asked myself the obvious question,

"What if she told someone? What if the police are on their way for me? Besides, she wouldn't dare do something as stupid as that."

I gazed out the window at all the passers-by in their nice suits and shiny shoes. Not only that, but whenever I found myself gazing outside a window, it always seemed as though I was trapped in something or trapped somewhere. I wondered if they had any secrets in their closets; I wondered if we could swap shoes to walk the next mile.

I needed a plan, a plan that would get me out of the mess I was in. In short, I had now realised where I had been going wrong – that if only I had searched for help earlier, the mess wouldn't have turned into a tragic story. Furthermore, I needed to break free from this chain of bondage tied around my neck like a noose around the hanged.

I left the messages unread and the missed calls unreturned for as long as possible, mainly because I would have no answer for the questions that would indeed be fired my way. I ran away from the one I love, consequently giving the win to the voice.

"I'm doing fine," I paused, trying to conjure up the perfect response. "My head was in a shambles and I just needed some time alone." Those were the words my nervous fingers allowed me to type.

It wasn't long after I hit the send button that my phone rang. It was Nicole, of course. I reassured her that I was fine before pressing the red button. I noticed a text from Rob that read: "Meet up at my house at six o'clock," it said.

I looked at the clock, and noticed that it said 15:00.

I replied with a simple "ok," which meant I was on my way.

The sun was blazing once more, causing my eyes to narrow in and in an attempt to focus, I searched for my sunglasses but was unsuccessful in finding them. I pulled up to Rob's house. It wasn't the first time I had been to his place, but each time I reached the front door it showed me something different. This time it was a gnome; it had a big white beard and a silver pointy hat - Rob was always a strange one for collecting little things.

I rang the doorbell that played a tune that reminded me of Christmas. It was a sweet melody, so I pressed it again before he opened the door. Rob answered the door with a cold beer in his hand.

"Hey," he said.

He seemed a bit excited to see me, so I allowed him to play on without asking why. I didn't want to be rude; after all, I guess he was trying to help and cheer me up, but I didn't have anything to be cheerful about.

"Come in," he finally said, inviting me into his beautiful home.

His house was in a beautiful neighbourhood, the posh side of London. All the homes around this side of town were well looked after, and that matched the price: it was big; in fact, it was about five times the size of my home. His wife is a lawyer, so obviously, they were loaded. They were childless therefore, free and certainly enjoyed an adrenalin-filled life in which they would occasionally take ski trips, tour Africa and the Caribbean; they had it all. But he was my friend, so sometimes he would take me on one of the trips, just like the one we had coming up.

It wasn't long after I had stepped through the front door that the fragrance of lime and lavender tickled my nose.

"Weird mix," I thought without questioning it. As a result, it caused me to sneeze, and a voice said "bless you" in the near distance.

"Thank you," I replied.

It was his wife, Tina.

"How's Nicole?" she asked.

"Fine," I said as if to suggest no further questions, please.

Tina was a good lawyer; she was a master at getting information out of someone. She was only a small woman in height, but what she lacked in size, she certainly had in intelligence. It made me wonder what she was doing with a guy like Rob. Not that she could do any better, it was just those kinds of people who like to stick together. Regardless, I smiled at her and followed Rob to the man cave.

'The sanctuary' as he called it, there was a bookcase on one of the walls. Half was filled with books while the other half was filled with games, computer games. He was able to dip from being a total gamer to being Sherlock Holmes. That was one thing we shared in common; we loved to read, and we equally loved Shakespeare. I directed my eyes over to the classic Romeo and Juliet and then I looked back over to him, seated in his favourite chair.

"Have you ever wondered what the story would have been like if they had lived and went on to have a family?" he looked at me, confused.

"What?" he asked.

"Romeo and Juliet," I answered.

"Oh them," he continued, "I never really thought about it. I guess it would be a happy ending," he concluded.

I took a seat opposite him on a small sofa.

"Nicole said you were missing last night: what happened?" he asked inquisitively.

I sighed out a sound that suggested nothing happened. I wanted to tell him, but I needed to allow my body and all its organs just to lay there as the distress was still flowing through my bloodstream. I finally let the words gush out like a dam held back, and I explained everything to him, telling him what I almost did and the crime I committed, holding my head down in shame, expecting a tirade of judgement, but there was none. Rob understood; after all, he knew me better than anyone.

"What if she tells Nicole?" he asked, "Or worse, what if she knows already?"

My heart sank at the thought. I asked: "What do you mean what if she knows?"

Rob looked away as if the question was too hard to answer,

"I mean, what if she knew what her sister did to you?"

I shook my head and closed my mouth; no more words were to come out.

"So what's the plan now?" he asked, standing up from his seat and pacing around the room like he was flicking through a book of solutions.

"Does anyone else know about last night?" he asked, ceasing his feet from any more movement.

"No," I replied, "furthermore, not even Nicole knows about this; she is pregnant and I don't want her to stress."

"What?" Rob interrupted, bringing his left foot to his right to maintain balance.

"Did you say she is pregnant?" he asked for clarity as his eyes peered over his glasses, waiting for an answer. "When was you going to tell me this?" he continued, still not allowing me to answer.

"Everything has been happening so fast, you wasn't told because it slipped my mind," I stood up to meet his eye level. "You know you're going to be the godfather, right?" I asked while telling him at the same time, "Due to your big house and fancy stuff, my child is sure to be well looked after if I'm dead."

We both laughed; a rare moment for me, but it was welcomed. Rob stopped his heavy chuckle that sounded like a fast car coming down the road and said, "I know a guy that can possibly help you, well, he's my wife's friend. He specialises in brain mental health, how the mind works and all that stuff. I will give him a call and set up a meeting for you. It's quite a while away but I think it might be worth your while."

Rob stepped out of the room, and it felt like he had been gone for an hour, but on checking the clock, it had only been ten minutes. He came back in with a smile on his face.

"Tomorrow," he blurted out, "the guy said he is able to squeeze you in tomorrow."

I smiled, not because I was happy at the speed at which I got the appointment, but because I had reached the point where I had nowhere else to turn but to get help. It was changing me,

"He will be expecting you so make sure you go no matter what," he warned, then picked up a snooker cue. "Come," he said, "come get your ass handed to you."

The time had come and I was dressed to impress. I wasn't much of a fashion icon, but I threw something together, and it looked nice. Okay, Nicole picked it out for me. She took one look at what I had chosen and calmly put the colour-clashed clothes back in the closet. She had left for work by the time I woke up.

I was once again on my way, flying down the weak set of stairs rushing as usual. I reached Paddington just in the nick of time. The train was ready to go as the last call was announced. I wasn't the only one running late; it was clear the woman on my left was running for the same reason. Her overly large breast swung from side to side. She looked at me for a brief moment as if she was telling me she couldn't run any more. I focused my gaze on the target, the train door. Without a doubt, I made it, and so did she. I found a seat near the window because nothing less would have done.

"Besides, what am I getting myself into?" I asked.

The train made a jerk; simultaneously, the sound of metal striking metal became a constant beat as we left Paddington station. I noticed an elder lady seated a few seats down the front; she seemed to be alone. She sat nearer to the aisle away from the window. Her hands were rolled into a fist, interlaced, and rested in her lap. Her knees bounced nervously as if they suggested meeting someone on the other end.

"Maybe a husband," I thought, "or maybe her children."

Her gaze looked distant, like her body was present, but her soul was elsewhere. I wanted to approach her.

"Give people a chance," Rob's voice echoed in my ear, "not everyone is the same."

I won the battle and kept seated. Above all, could Rob's doctor friend help? My voice pitched, so I dug down into my bag in search of water. Eyes watched my every move like I was about to pull out a gun and I was confused, and then it hit me; the bombing that had happened the previous week had placed everyone on suspicion mode, and this added fuel to their already stereotypical, judgemental point of view. The world was on the edge of its seat, and no one trusted anyone. Husbands and wives checked each other's phones, colleagues told on each other, everyone was viewed with a title above their heads: thief, pervert, racist, and I guess mine was terrorist.

"Things are only going to get worse," I thought to myself while taking several sips of the water.

Eyes looked away as I caught them. Many believed that the government orchestrated the bombings to instil and keep fear alive, and in many ways, I thought, *fear is a tool and a powerful one at that...It controls and drives a particular motives. In the hands of the powerful, it's not something to go up against.* I snapped out of my thoughts and peeped through the grooves of the seats.

I noticed that the old lady was still sitting by herself; it bugged me that she was alone. All of a sudden, I started to care and it was like a thorn in my side prompting me to get up. Her energy pulled and vibrated along with the same frequency as mine and because of this, I made my way to the toilet. I didn't need to go, but I wanted an excuse to cross her path - there was just something, I couldn't quite put my finger on it, but I felt compelled. On the way back, the train threw me from side to side, and she looked up at me with a worried glance. I gestured to her, and it was an awkward smile met with a more pleasant one as she returned a 'good morning'.'

I shakily wandered back to my seat; her composure was unmatched, her folded interlaced fist was still in her lap; her mind was still somewhere else. It seemed she only snapped out to say good morning to me. Something wasn't right, I thought, and therefore I got up, went over, and sat beside her. She didn't mind smiling at me as I climbed over to sit by the window. I turned to start a conversation with her, but each time I turned, she was forward-facing and didn't seem like she wanted to talk. Her eyes didn't move.

"Is she a machine?" I thought. "Was she sent to spy on me?" I wondered.

On the third attempt, I went for it: "Hey," I said as the words left my mouth, shaking.

It wasn't like I was trying to chat her up; she just intrigued me. After all, she was at least two or more times my age. At the least, the conversation picked up as we discussed general topics, the weather, the train. I quickly broke the boring cycle and asked her what brought her there that day? The old lady, whose name is Dorothy, said she was visiting her late husband's grave.

"He committed suicide 5 years ago today," she said with a calmness in her tone, but my heart sunk.

My eyes watered instantly; no tears fell once more, but they watered and my mouth was dry and evil tasting as I thought of the voice.

"Ooh no," I replied as the train took a nose dive down the hilly track.

The train entered a tunnel as the conversation took a pause. It was dark, both inside and out, the lights in the train had stopped working.

My reflection turned to someone unrecognisable, and it didn't look like me. My body temperature went up to at least one-fifty, and the train fell silent. I looked around to check if everyone was asleep, but I couldn't see through the thickness of the dark and so I turned and looked at Dorothy, undoubtedly and right on time, a feeling of guilt coming to me.

"She must be feeling lonely," I thought.

Clearly, the same fate was running away from me, and it had brought me within touching distance of what it looked like. I could taste her fear. Her energy was drained, thus explaining the minimal movement. I once contemplated doing the same thing.

"I felt and to a certain degree I still feel like I have no choice," I murmured.

I didn't want her to see my face, but the train exited the tunnel, and a soft lady voice over the P.A apologised for the blackout. As I continued to tell her about the voice in my head, she sustained her gaze to the front and didn't seem surprised by what I had said. It was like she knew the voice personally or maybe encountered a similar, if not the same, experience. She congratulated me for going to see the doctor, reminding me to tell him everything.

"Professional help is what would have saved my husband if only he wasn't so stubborn," she noted. "Get help," she concluded as if I didn't hear her the first time.

She went quiet for a while, mourning her late husband, it appeared. I left her to it and didn't say another word until she reached her stop. She whispered in my ear like she was trying to penetrate my drum to reach the voice.

"Remember your purpose in life, connect with people," she said, "I know there are bad people for the most part but give them a chance just like you did with me today. When you are at your lowest, remember your loved ones, remember you're loved, wanted and needed. The voice will always use your fears against you, but remember your fear is only an obstacle in the way of your greatness." She got up and walked to the exit.

"Don't think too hard," she shouted.

It was hardly a shout; it was as loud as it could get for a lady her age without hurting herself. I showed her just a smile in reply while raising my hand to say goodbye. The train left the station, and I looked down at my hands, which was only last night that they were around another lady's neck, fixing to end her life. I walked to the toilet, ran the hot water, and washed them clean - clean from the blood that would have been if I had squeezed harder.

My eyes were closed as the train jolted, alerting me of a stop. The same soft voice I heard earlier was mouthing something over the speakers.

"This is Menide station, please mind your step." The name rung a bell as I remembered the directions Rob gave me.

I grabbed my bag, took a couple of giant steps, and leaped off the train, leaving my water on the seat. I sighed as my eyes were still asleep, clearly lagging behind my brain being rebooted. I looked up at the fluorescent lights leading me towards the taxi stand.

The taxi pulled up outside the address. I looked at the address and then at the building through the murky windows.

"Are you sure this is the right place?" I asked the driver.

"Ay, my friend," he replied in a thick northern accent, "this is where the satnav took us."

The building was a one storey shack-looking piece. It lacked attention and was in need of TLC. It had a peaked roof resembling a church. A sign outside read, 'master your mind.'

"What in the hell has Rob sent me across the country for?" I murmured to myself behind my clenched teeth.

Despite my lack of trust and enthusiasm, I dragged my feet towards the entrance and walked through the door. A young lady greeted me. She was stunning, beautiful brown skin with her hair out in an afro style. Her eyes caught me staring at her while she spoke. I didn't understand a word of what she said. Her accent was equally as strong as the taxi driver's, except that she was beautiful. If she had continued talking any longer, I would have been drooling. I asked her for Dr. Crawford. She took my name and asked me to take a seat in the waiting area. The inside of the building was quite a contrast from the outside.

"Very misleading," I added while rocking my head in admiration.

Many pictures accompanied the wall, and each picture had a caption written underneath. Some of the pictures were thought-provoking, to say the least—one of them, a picture of a man's face. The photo was fuzzy, almost like a smoke machine was in front of him. His visibility was limited; only his eyes and the outlines of his shoulders were made out. He had a straight face, not smiling but not sad either. I didn't know where he was born, where he died or not. Then my eyes caught the caption at the bottom; it asked, "how did it feel when your soul left your body?"

I reread the caption, this time slower than the first, "How did it feel when your soul left your body?"

I realised he was dead by the small RIP written at the bottom. My eyes broke contact with the picture as my thoughts carried on looking. Many people lose their souls without dying.

"There," called the pretty lady who stood up from her desk and approached me.

She interrupted my thought by the way she placed one foot in front of the other. She reminded me of a model.

"The Dr will see you now," she said seductively. It wasn't sexual; it was a command.

I entered the Dr's room. It was warm, cozy, bright, and filled with more of those pictures from outside. The man that greeted me was a small man.

"A lot smaller than me," I thought, especially when I shook his hand.

"What is this place?" I thought, still not knowing where Rob had sent me. The Dr introduced himself as Dr. Crawford.

"Take a seat," he said casually.

I couldn't get used to the accent; it was so difficult that each word that stopped at the door of my ears took fifteen seconds to comprehend. There was a desk located in the corner of the room. Not where you would expect a desk to be, by the window, looking out at the world on a beautiful sunny day, but in a corner like he was running away from that very idea of beauty. In the middle of the room were two soft chairs, one longer than the other. The chairs looked bizarre.

"Once you're in my room I have two rules: smile and smile some more," he declared.

It looked like he was joking, so I gave a half-smile.

He went on, "I understand that you have been having some difficulties."

I nodded.

"I have spoken to your friend Robert, he briefly filled me in on the situation. Take a seat please," he added as if he had forgotten his manners. "Can you shed some light on your darkness?" he said, tilting his equally small glasses towards the tip of his nose to look at me.

"Not only that," referring to the darkness, I jumped in, allowing my words to express the trauma from the first time it happened to the more recent crime. I spared no details. The Dr sat on the edge of his seat, listening intently as he shuffled to and fro. I finished the story as the Dr took over, asking me many questions about my childhood, my earliest memory of pain, love, and laughter. He quizzed me deeply, and his questions annoyed me as they seemed trivial and motionless, prompting me to jump to my feet with my fist clenched.

"You're the one supposed to give me the answers!" I shouted, "I've come all this way and all you've done is ask me questions after questions, I was starting to sound like the voice."

The base in my voice alerted the pretty young lady to shuffle in her seat, but she recomposed herself as I watched her behind the blurred glass separating the office from the waiting area. The voice was not in my head at that time; it was all me. It was too late, I thought. I was more than halfway across to the dark side. The Dr looked at me with a smile.

"Take a seat," he calmly said.

It was definitive that his sheer composure and experience kept the situation storm-free. The session continued for a further hour, and by the end of it, I was lighter. The Dr was a genius, I resigned to say, I left that room with a smile on my face. The Dr went through a plan of action with me,

"Fear," he said, fixing his glasses on the bridge of his nose once more, "fear is what keeps you down, stops you from maintaining a level of sanity. It robs you of your joy and peace," he continued, "you also need to join a group and talk to like-minded people to find more intricate ways to help. And by the way," he concluded, "give people a chance, the world ain't such a bad place as you so eloquently described it. Call back in a week and let me know how you're getting on and then we will book you back in another month for an update chat."

I agreed, feeling full of life, shook his hands, apologised for my outburst, and left.

CHAPTER 10

By 6a.m. the following morning, light had eliminated darkness and night had turned into day. The morning routine became the most important; it set the mood for whatever was to come. The floor became a place where I could rest my mind and allow it to drift away to a place where the world was a better place. That morning, I was entangled in a meditative stance, my feet crossed as my eyes gently locked and I felt like I was floating. It was real, and no one could have told me differently - I was a butterfly that went where I wanted, cutting through the wind with a flutter of my wings. I wasn't the birds from my window, but I got my wish; I was happy, free, and at peace.

Soft, mellow instrumentals accompanied my ears as I sat motionlessly. My heart was filled with wishes and dreams of betterment. I needed to strengthen my mind, and I had to follow the doctor's orders. They were precise and direct, and I needed to be at one with myself.

"Learn to control your mind," he had said, "allow the thoughts to enter and exit your mind without giving them a second thought." "Practice that and you will notice considerable differences," he had concluded.

I trusted him, so I listened; that was the best I had ever felt from the day I took my first gasp of fresh air after exiting the bubble that wrapped me in the womb. I was watering the right thoughts, paying attention to the things that would last, my mind. The cool breeze blew through the open kitchen window, undoubtedly interrupting my search for joy as the curtains swayed side to side, revealing a man outside on his balcony. He wore purple swim shorts, and his overly large stomach was round enough to pop with a pin. He's the last thing you wanted to see so early in the morning. He sang a tune I could only explain as horrid. If I was any closer, my ears would bleed, not only that but my eyes too. I closed the window, ending the nightmare. Nicole was still asleep, so I went into the shower. The clock struck seven.

Knock! Knock! Was the sound of delicate fingers crashing against the bathroom door.

"Hurry up!" the crackled morning voice broke the silence.

"I'm almost done!" I shouted over the sound of the water smashing against the floor. "I'll be out soon," I repeated as the *knock* continued.

"Her ears must still be tuned in to the dream from last night," I wondered, assuming she dreamt.

"Good morning baby," I announced on the way out.

She grinned as I kissed her, grabbing her bum as I stepped to the side. I wanted to marry her there and then; the wait was too long and my love for her kept on growing, and she didn't know it. Expressing it had become difficult; the voice had filled every inch of space in my dome and he left no room for anyone else; he wanted me for himself.

"He's gone now, so she will know how much I love her," I danced around the living room with a towel around my waist. The joy in my joints bubbled and allowed extra flexibility. I texted Rob and told him to meet me at the gym.

"It's time for a session," I joked, pumped and ready to let off some steam.

"It's been a while," I thought as the grin on my face progressed into a smile.

I pulled up to the gym with the windows down and sun glasses on, parked the car and was ready to exit when my phone rang. I had just opened the car door and had one leg already out. The call was from an unknown number, thus prompting me to be skeptical. I answered gingerly without saying hello as the voice caught me off guard due to the recognisable tongue.

"Hey," I whispered, breaking silence.

"How are you doing?" the voice on the other end countered, and the conversation continued for a further ten minutes as I warmed to the sound of the voice on the other end. It was Lisa, and I left the conversation smiling as it was a someone that was genuinely checking up on me. Although her lack of control with regards to her gossiping was annoying, it was still a good feeling to have her call me. I gave her no information but instead kept it short sweet and simple - she still wasn't to be trusted.

A thunderous voice from the other end of the car park shouted, "Andreas, come on." The figure stood by the entrance of the gym waving his hand as if he was in a crowd at a festival: it was Rob. "I have been waiting for the last five minutes," he continued to shout. I laughed - not hysterically, just to myself.

"Let's go," he demanded. "We are not going to the gym today," he said. I was confused and scared at the same time; Rob was always on the hunt for the next crazy so I didn't know what to expect. "We are going for a long run," he said, ending my worries.

"That's OK," I confirmed, putting on my running shoes. Behind the gym is a football and rugby pitch, we done laps of the field, ten laps I think - the counting got left behind as the pain in my feet and the stitch in my stomach took centre stage. We ran and struggled to talk: "How - was - the – meeting?" Rob asked as he took a sharp breath after each word.

"It - was - really - good," I replied as I was equally unsuited for that kind of workout. We continued to run and struggle to talk, and although the drill was hard, we completed it. There was a football match being played as we finished, and we took the invitation from the benches and sat down. It was a beautiful feeling. "I spoke with the doctor," Rob mentioned. He told me how the session went: "He thinks highly of you," he continued, "he believes that you will get better, a lot sooner than you think, and he just encouraged me to support you the best I can." Rob put his hand on my shoulder as if he was congratulating or encouraging me.

"The meditations in the morning has been a heaven sent," I added, "something that I would never had given a second thought has been a game changer in my life and I'm able to free my mind and set my goals from the morning." Rob cracked a smile, bringing his mouth away from the water bottle he had been sipping on.

"It's something me and my wife try to do on a regular basis," he affirmed, "along with Yoga," he added, escalating his voice to to make sure I had heard him.

"Obviously," I laughed, this time out loud as control went out of the window, "you and your fat self," I jumped in with an insult. The players closest to us looked over as if they wanted to laugh also. "How's that possible?" I asked, still laughing. It was never personal whenever I insulted him; most times he would laugh with me. This time his reply was not that of laughter, but something to really ponder. He said ignorance is paradise. "Paradise," I whispered, not being able to connect the dots to understand. "Yes," he replied, "don't get comfortable and caught up in what you think you know," he explained. I felt like a school child being told off by the head master. We stayed on the bench until the life in our legs came back as we watched the game and commentated like we knew and could do any better. It was fun. "Next week," I said, reminding Rob of the trip planned, and we got up and left the field.

It didn't take me long to reach home. I parked the car along a side road not too far away from my flat but I had to do some more walking. "Great," I murmured to myself as I grabbed my bag from the boot and slung it round my shoulders. A man in a big blue jacket was walking towards me; he seemed somewhat disorientated, but I thought nothing of it. As he got closer he looked me in the eye, and the look frightened me at first because his eyes were bloodshot like he was on something. We reached within touching distance and he looked away then back at me, stopping in front of me and blocking my way, looked dead in my eyes as I stared back at him, my mind was telling me it was about to go down. We was about to scrap; I was ready, the blood from the run was still pumping through my veins. He continued to stare at me without saying a word - he was testing me. It seemed like my peace was too good to be true, maybe the voice had sent someone to disrupt my life once more, maybe he hadn't forgotten that I betrayed him. I had the feeling again that someone was following me, and I looked around to make sure. *Was he in hiding, waiting for the perfect moment to strike?* I wasn't sure; all I cared about was here and now, my fist clenched and if I had to fight for my life or my belongings. I was ready to do so as with a swift but unusual slide of his hand he took his hood off and asked me for the time. It was so weird; I had never seen anything like that in my life - he most definitely was on something. The stench from his direction told me what he had been up to; he wasn't homeless, I could tell by the clothes he was wearing - it was all designers - he was a well-off guy by the looks of it. I told him the time and swiftly side-stepped him and carried on walking home. I gave a slight look back, just to make sure he wasn't behind me.

It would soon be dark and I had decided to have Nicole meet me at a corner of Croker's Street, it was date night – a night that filled us with expectation. The voice wouldn't dare ruin a night like this with his intrusive unwelcome self. This is supposed to be special.

I grabbed my phone, peered through the rather blurry window of the car and dialled.

"Hey babes," was the greeting that echoed from my lips when she picked up. "Are you ready? Meet me at Crocker's Street Corner. I'm all ready. Just park across the street and I'll come to you." she ended.

I welled up with pride whilst she walked towards the car, and I got out to admire her as she strutted like that of a fashion show looking like the million dollar prize that I had won. That purple dress was like a wallpaper that would serve as the background to our date tonight. It made me feel like back when I was dating her and we weren't living together as yet. I was smiling from ear to ear while walking to meet her. I caught her in my arms as I hugged and squeezed her.

"Hey," she responded giggling as if she was embarrassed. Her hand was behind her head, still tying her hair. "How was your day?" she asked, her purple dress flowing as I spun her around, and if the cameras were rolling we would have gotten the role as lovers in a romantic story. I let go of her waist and placed my hands on her growing stomach, nothing was kicking as yet but I know someone special was in there; the scan was due next week and the wedding was in three weeks' time. *A lot happening at once,* I thought; still, it was a great time for me, I reminded myself.

"Are you ready?" I asked.

"Of course," she replied with excitement in her voice, "I've been ready all day."

"We're not going to a concert," I announced and we both giggled like we were back at school. I looked at her with a cheeky smile on my face - it reminded me of the first time we met, the fun we had, the dates we went on, the adventures we got ourselves into. I opened the car door for Nicole like the gentleman I am, then skipped around to the driver's side. The man from earlier was back; this time he walked straight past me, still looking unwell, the hood covering his pale, patchy skin was now down and it was more apparent: what was he still doing on the road? I asked myself. I climbed into the car and asked Nicole if she saw him.

"No, what guy?" she questioned.

"Nothing," I responded. "I thought I saw someone." I ended as we drove off to hand the car back to the dealership.

The night shone like the Tokyo strip and the heat from the neon signs brought shadows alive as with each step we took they accompanied us with a sense of life, fulfilment and joy; it felt like we were in a pixilated movie and we were the stars. It was like we were stepping into each spot of light in the light, hoping to encounter better, more enriched level of being, rather than just existing, and at that moment we looked at each other and smiled. A flash came out of nowhere, and another one, then followed by a request for five dollars. Someone had captured our moment and wanted to sell it back to us, a true example of capitalism. We shook our heads and walked off; the moment was perfect, in spite of the opportunist it was heaven and I was floating like a butterfly again, not because of love but because of being free, and in that moment everything was right, right where it needed to be, right where it was intended. We continued to walk, gazing up at all the wondrous lights that directed our path - *Splash*, was the sound my large feet made as they plunged into the puddle on the floor. I made a growl as if I had bucked my toe on the bed side table and I paused for a second as if I was waiting on the timely arrival of the inhumane savage, but he didn't appear as my sense of feeling kicked in and registered that my whole feet were wet, water had filled my socks, shoes and half way up my trouser leg; it was a thickish liquid, with a bad odorous smell, similar to that of boil mixed with pigs guts.

"Oh no!" gasped Nicole with a slight giggle on her face. I caught her in the side of my eye. I was fuming but it had to hold my composure, the night was going so well I couldn't let this ruin it for the both of us, so I laughed with her, the laugh coming out like I had just eaten the hottest of peppers, awkward. She looked up, looking for somewhere to dry my feet - that place looks decent enough to have a blow dryer in their toilet. She pointed with a grumble coming out of her mouth, and I shook my head in disbelief one last time as I took small steps towards the refuge offered to me and hopped on the good leg the whole way there, almost stumbling on my face and calling it a night, as if I had just received an injury from football. My feet felt warm, and a freakish feeling travelled up my leg as it registered one cold and one warm, and it brought chills up my body. I walked out of the cafe to meet my lady like a scene from a James Bond film, and we connected and were ready to continue our night. We directed our motion over to a place called Rustles.

"A real meat lovers dream," I said as my stomach grumbled. The place was filled with all different types of meat, from the ordinary grilled chicken to the outrageous grilled donkey

"I'll give that one a miss," she replied. "The place is well known and has won a variety of awards; many people have also died of heart attack," she so blatantly said.

"We must try it," I said as I asked with the same breath, "we must live," I blurted out as I noticed a little glimmer of doubt in the white of her eye. I didn't want her to ruin it for me. When we got there the place was rammed pack, queue stretched all the way outside; the place was busy. We waited and were told forty five minutes by the hostess.

"It will be worth the wait," I gingerly said without giving her eye contact. Her eyes were sharp enough to convince a cat to come down from a tree, her face painted a picture of impatience, and I noticed her eyes rolling at the prospect of the lengthy wait, but reluctantly she obliged and we waited at the bar, ordering a pint of cold beer, and a glass of orange juice for the lady. We sipped and talked, time passing as we were called to take our seats. I rubbed my hands together as a child would upon arriving at a buffet, and I devoured my meal and left only the chewed up bones, the hairs at the back of my neck prickling up as I sucked the juices out, licked my lips and let out a soft discrete belch.

The moonlight graced the rest of our evening as we walked along a closed park, we enjoyed walking as it allowed us to talk, hold hands and be close. The darkness of the night hugged us to the point that we could barely see each other despite being no more than a foot away, something that hardly happens on the Tokyo strip. The park had no lights - we had stepped from the light and into the darkness. I laughed to myself as if it was a true reflection of how things were going.

"The wedding was once again the hot topic and honeymoon destinations," she said. As the suggestions of Portugal came up, the Caribbean, Asia and all destinations out of our price range, I reminded her, bringing her high flying wish crashing to the floor. We continued the subject matter until we reached the end of the park and street lights were out continuing the theme of pure darkness. Only the car lights lit up the roads.

"The bus is coming," shouted Nicole as she shot in its direction. The bus driver looked in no mood to wait around. *Finishing his shift to go home to his family*, I thought. Nicole shot across the road and was stunned by a fast approaching car. The car was about ten seconds away from her as she froze in the middle of the road, revealing a daunting fate.

"Nine seconds - look out," I shouted at her, causing everyone else to look around in fear of what was about to happen. *Eight seconds*, I counted in my head as I froze also, Nicole was not moving and I wished for her to move her feet out of the car's way. The car was braking so hard it started to squeak its tyres and - *seven seconds*, she still had time to move. My mind shifted to our unborn child: if it is a boy, I thought, I would name him Carlos and if it's a girl I would name her Trinity. *Four seconds*... the car was now swerving uncontrollably. I could see the guy in the car, young, maybe in his twenties if not younger. He was trying but he wasn't in control of her fate, it was written in the big book a long time ago. *Three seconds…* I called out to her one last time, but her eyes were closed like a deer at the mercy of headlights, like she knew she had no chance. *Two seconds…* I had no choice but to join her; if she was going then so was I. I begged the driver for an ounce of leniency or perhaps charity, whatever he could offer. I just wanted him to stop. My eyes narrowed as though that would have altered the inevitable or take the pain away. I sent a prayer up asking for mercy not knowing to whom it was going to but hoping it would touch someone's heart string, someone divine and all powerful. The car stopped, revealing the driver with both hands on the steering wheel, who looked as scared as we were as the car stopped a meter away from us. Nicole was already out of tears as she cried a wordless howl, opening her eyes as death ceased the knocking at her door. I picked her up and carried her to safety as her legs were still shaking. The bus driver and all his passengers watched in panic and fear, not knowing whether they would bear witness to life being taken or another chance of redemption being handed out. The bus driver opened the door as we walked up to complete what we intend to do. I boarded the bus with Nicole in my arms. *She shivered, or was it me?* I wondered. I wasn't sure, but I know it wasn't nerve, it was discomposure wrapped in a mess of uneasiness. We took a seat locked in each other's arms and then the bus drove off with a voice saying, *"You should have left her, you don't know who she is".*

CHAPTER 11

It was three days after Nicole had stared in the eyes of death and come out the other end smiling; one wonderful soul spared from the merciless jaws of the grim reaper. "Life is too short", I mumbled to myself as the idea of losing my one true love dawned on me. Loneliness would have overpowered me right there and then, swallowed me up and melted me in the acid of its stomach. My head dropped at the thought of how it would have been and the rising of the sun wasn't enough to burn away the feelings.

Once again I found myself a slave to her graceful movement as she moved around the kitchen, my eyes her untiring admirer.

"Look at her," I said to myself as I made note of her pureness. I was the luckiest man in the whole world. I thought for a moment about the day we met, the day she said *yes* and the day the universe saved her life. She was getting ready to meet her sister, not the wicked one.

I moved my backside in the sofa as if I was uncomfortable, except I was deep in thought and as a consequence I got lost in the realm of the universe bouncing from star to star. My mind was becoming somewhat distorted, fuzzy and delusional, but the ten percent of me that was still sane had the courage to rub my eyes and snap out of the quick sand prompting me to spring to my feet. I turned around to glance at the mirror only to find the image staring back at me unfamiliar as it wasn't clear - it was as though I was fading or faded away. It seemed like I was on a timer and I had limited time to grab hold of what was left of me. The hazy face in the mirror seemed to be smiling back at me. *That's not me*, I tried to convince myself. My head filled with blood as it rushed to the areas pounding, and my memory went, and I didn't know where I was. I rubbed my eyes again as if a cloud was blocking my view whilst my head got tighter and the pain moved from left to right then to the front. "The curse that has followed me trying to steal my companionship has resurrected!" my voice took a dramatic turn; it was like I was in a theatre performance playing the role of my life. *It can't be*, I thought without allowing the words to leave my mouth. The feeling haunted me with the voice I murmured taking a long pause and my body shivered like I was in an ice box. Nicole glided along the floor in a quick motion and the sound she created was like that of a cat's long nails clattering on the ground. She looked in my hollow eyes and asked if I was okay. She looked concerned, as though she recognised the stare. I was still shaking, clearly disturbed, so I looked over at the window to see if it was open, my eyes connected with the hole-in-the-wall as the sound of a prison door slamming echoed in my head. The window was closed so I focused back on Nicole as my mouth opened, "He's back!"

The following day we were invited to a family function. Nicole's mother was turning sixty and the whole family was planning on surprising her. Nicole informed me that everyone was going to be there but I wasn't totally sure if she meant absolutely everyone. The hate circled the veins of my eyes as I looked up at her, hoping she didn't mean to reconnect with her eldest sister. We both agreed that we would meet up later at the family's house.

She suggested jubilantly as she gathered her purse, "I have a few things I need to do, nails I thought, hair maybe." I couldn't think straight the empty spaces in my head were already filled by nothing healthy I noted. We kissed and departed on our separate ways. The school had been calling me that day and so they left messages saying I should come in for an evaluation because they wanted to see if I was fit enough to go back to work. I shook my head and thought of yesterday. "I am in no shape to be signed off," I declared as I paced around the room looking for something to smash. I spent all that time trying to recover and it may all be in vain - the voice may still be flowing through my system collaborating with each of my organs to turn against me. The meditation had been helping; I did it every day from the day the doctor said, and now the feeling that I felt in my body was a lot stronger than I had experienced before. It felt stronger and more intense, and I didn't know if I was ready to handle it if he came back to haunt me.

The dusty black cab dropped me at the front gate as it rattled and squeaked in all the unexpected areas. The price I paid didn't match up to the service I had received but I had no choice but to sit there and hope for the best as the cockney driver peered his large red cheeks against the Perspex separating us.

"That'll be twenty-three fifty," he announced, prompting me to search the already deep pockets of my jeans.

The music was playing, as I could hear it out on the road. The lights in the house clearly reflected the guests having a good time. The smell of food made me take a deep breath and the sound of music made my feet happy as I walked up to the front of the house, obviously noticing the ever-beautiful flowers that had been carefully planted in ways only pride could explain. The wooden front door had always creaked as it swung on an ancient hinge that her mother didn't want to change. "Nicole's mother never liked changing the old, she said everything that held this house together was precious, valuable and useful. *Maybe she was making an indirect reference to herself,* I pondered. I pushed with the strength and delicateness of a child as if I was sneaking in. I didn't want to alert anybody of my arrival. I wanted to go in, find Nicole, and greet her mother then leave, definitely in that order, I confirmed. It wasn't because her family didn't like me. In fact, they loved me but I just wasn't in the mood to talk or to be around anyone or to even hear their stories of how their days have been and what was new in their lives because I just didn't care. My plan however failed when the door made the loudest noise it had ever made. I dropped my chin to centre of my chest as disappointment filled me. The dancers on the floor looked over their shoulders as if police had kicked the door down as they gave me a smile as if to say *come in.*

"Hey," they said as I walked past. I gave them the usual smile along with a casual *hey*. Did I mean it? No, but I wasn't going to cause a scene - not in front of her family. Nicole saw me from across the room as my face lit up in alignment with hers. "Hi, hello," was the tune playing from my mouth for the next five minutes. I was settled in now.

"Do you want a drink?" she asked softly in my ears over the tone of the music. I ignored the offer unintentionally as I spotted her mother in the corner of the room. A faint smile twitched the corner of my face as I danced my way over to wish her a happy birthday. She was always happy to see me and she wrapped her chubby arms around me squeezing the life away. She admitted I was the best thing for her daughter and certainly the best man she has ever brought home. I released the tight hug I had graced her with and she did the same and we stood in the same spot talking for a while until Nicole called me over. She tried again with the drink offer and it was a success this time.

"A glass of cider please," I asked as I got into the groove. My mood was now different compared to an hour ago because the sight of Nicole always changed things. The cider had a little influence as well; I was now enjoying the night, the party was in full swing and I was sweating as I danced my way around the whole house greeting the rest of the family. Her father was absent since he left her and her mother when Nicole was only nine and never to be seen again. *His loss,* I thought as

I fixed my gaze on what he is missing out on. Her eyes watched me back with a delicious smile. The crowd got larger as the room filled with friends and family not *much space to move* I worried, "fire risk". I mumbled as my anxiety got the better part of me.

The door creaked again while I moved every part of my body to the beat. Kris Kross played that night - an old-time classic, my favourite. The figure that walked through the door looked familiar, the sort of familiar that you didn't want to see again. The door opened wider causing deathly fragrance to swirl in my nostrils. It burned the rim of my nose as it felt like the air had melted. The beat of the music left the room causing me to move and hunt it down. I was no longer able to dance as my feet had frozen and was now sinking in sand somewhere in a desert. I was sweating in larger amounts and I felt sad again - as if I had dropped my ice cream and watched it melt - and I felt as though someone was on my back holding me down. They were strong and bullish; except there was no one there - the sensation of someone holding me came from the memory of the guard holding me as a little boy, but I was still motionless with my arms glued to my side. My head however was fixed on the person coming through the door. It was a lady and her face was a little blurry, and for a moment I thought that the drinks I had been gulping were the cause for this effect but as she drew closer, the image got clearer. Her face was fuzzy like the image that peered back at me yesterday. The balls in the socket of my skull scanned the room flitting timorously from face to face trying to lock on to the mystery lady. My tongue felt like it was swollen like a puffer fish and I wasn't able to move it to articulate words. I fell dumb as the figure went up the stairs and out of line of vision. I tried my hardest to move my feet but it wasn't until the next song had started that I was able to free myself. The sensation in my leg was tingling and I fell face first as if I was a child again trying to walk. Only a few people helped me to my feet. I wasn't embarrassed and I didn't care even though I had fallen.

My head and eyes were fixed on the stairs and who went up there. My body was in my control again as I took off after the spirit up the stairs. My legs were however moving like a motor on drugs. Up I went, checking every room for the figure or at least a trace of stain left by mistake but no one was there. No stain, nothing. I changed gear again as I ran down the stairs skipping two then three steps to reach the bottom.

"Did she invite her sister?" I asked myself, looking perplexed and confused. "It couldn't be." I said while picking my jaw up from the floor. I was pretty sure I saw her. I dug the pits of my memory, making sure I was not going crazy but unfortunately, the pit was empty for I had no reference and I'm sure no one else had seen what I saw. It scared me and made me panic. I did tell her what I would do if I saw her again and I meant it. I should just kill her and throw her body in the river, that'll make sure I don't see her again. It was a thought that crossed my mind a while ago but I didn't want to entertain it. Fear is behind me now and she is in my way. I went back up the stairs slower than before and all the while noticing the family portraits on the wall. I washed my face in the face basin, dried it and went back down the stairs took a couple shots of *Wray and his Nephew* to drown out what had just happened as the night went on and followed the same mood. I couldn't enjoy myself and the time approached midnight as the clock struck twelve.

"Hello Andreas, remember me?" an iron voice from the back of my head announced. I turned around immediately to acknowledge the voice but there was no one there!

"Not this again!" I shouted knocking over the only drink I had to the floor. The music was still playing loud enough for pedestrians on the street to hear but in my head it was dead silent such that a pin drop was noticeable as I searched for the voice.

"Come out and let's finish this!" I challenged.

"It's either you or me," I warned.

"It will be somebody," he replied. His tone was soft and subtle. It was weird and his composure was unbearable. *Perhaps he had seen the future,* I thought as I made my way out of the house. The temperature had gone up again. I was well aware that it was summer but it felt like I was near a volcano that was erupting.

"Do you really think that you had gotten rid of me for the hundredth time?" he asked. Knowing the answer to the question, it was like he was sitting in the back of my head while I was bettering myself, laughing and planning at my attempts of freedom. "Remember when I told you I didn't want to hurt you? Well, that has changed now. I'm going to destroy you and everyone around you. I think I will start with the ones closest to you!" he laughed. It was evil as if the laugh was some kind of spell that blew you up from the inside. I wondered if the laugh was directed at God. I wondered if he would be scared and throw in the towel. "I made a promise to you," he continued, "I promised you that I would never leave you alone. I gave you a way out and you choose the wrong path!" the tone was now deep and it made him feel stronger like someone in authority he had control and it scared me. The rash on my arm had swollen up again and my finger nails met the rawness as it dug up some flesh. The voice was no longer at the back of my head but was now at the front, so close that it felt like he was looking out through my eyes and that he was breathing the same air. I pushed and bumped past the crowded living room and made my way back out of the front door and I was outside no longer feeling squashed and trampled on. I sucked in another load of fresh air as a result causing me to choke until I almost spat blood as I took motion up the road in the pitch darkness of the night. The darkness covered me fitting the role of a friend as I walked hard and fast into the unknown. Tears ran down my eyes like water from the edge of a river bed. My clothes were soaking wet filled with sweat or maybe blood but definitely tears. I looked homeless or like an irresponsible drunk. Surely, if I wasn't careful someone would have called the police and then into a nut house. I needed Nicole. My nose ran and she wasn't here to wipe it like that of a sick child. I stumbled as I walked grazing my palms along the ground.

"I have to end this," I stammered. "This cannot go on for much longer," I mumbled. The voice slammed my mouth shut with his bare hands and laughed as if he was watching a comedy show.

"You don't seem to understand," was the reminder I got. "You don't seem to understand that you are fighting a losing battle my friend," he said, as if we were close friends. I gathered myself and turned back and on my way to the house, and Nicole noticed me dragging my feet along the road, hoping a car was coming but none did. I looked beaten up as she ran to my rescue, holding and wiping my face. Sadness and loneliness was the weight I was carrying but it was getting too heavy as the voice threatened to take them away. I tried to hold on for as long as possible but I was weak.

Nicole's lips trembled as distorted words came out, "Is he back"? she asked.

"Yes," I nodded.

"Let's go!" she demanded. "Let's go home." She gathered her stuff, called a cab and we left without saying goodbye to the family.

The cool breeze blew through the cracks of the cab window, and it was cool on the inside, but not inside my head – inside my head it was still blazing with heat. I didn't want the driver to hear what was going on, so we spoke with limited tones and I sobbed in her arms as she tried to catch the tears before they fell to the ground. She hated that we were right back to this place again and she was now starting to get frustrated and annoyed. I looked at her, thinking, *If only you knew what it was like for a dark cloud to follow you, and sometimes striking lighting directly on top of your head.*

She turned away from me as if she also was able to hear my thoughts, her head in her hands and her hands in her lap. I looked at the driver through the glass and I heard him say, "today is your day." The statement was faint; it was quiet enough to evade Nicole's ears. "What did you say?" I shouted through the compact hole in the glass; I shouted it again, this time banging on the screen to get his attention. The voice kept on laughing and screaming, and my head hurt beyond pain - it was now numb. I banged on the glass several times without stopping. The driver was now shouting, but for some reason he didn't stop the cab but continued driving faster, swerving. In the distance was the fox I had hit, his eyes bulged out, tongue hanging. I gave the glass one last hit, causing it to crack.

"Holy shit!" cried the driver as the cab swayed left and then right causing the driver to slam on the brakes. In a moment of stillness, I noticed a fox still in the middle of the road – not dead, but walking towards me.

The driver clipped the edge of a tree losing control causing my head to slam against the side walls of the cab and glass shattered into my face. In all the madness I noticed Nicole was already on the floor of the cab, her hand on her stomach holding onto her bump as best she could. The cab rolled and rolled without stopping for money or love as I tried my best to stretch my hand out to hold on to her, but it wasn't working. A splash of blood slapped my cheeks, causing me to close my eyes briefly but before I could blink the second time the cab was wrapped around another tree it was in that moment of chaos I noticed a tree branch pierced right through the side of the cab and into Nicole's side. A pang of pain shot through my body as my head slammed against one of the pillars once more, almost knocking me out. An electric shock ran through my head and in that instance, I wished the shock would destroy the voice inside. The cab landed on top of its roof, bringing the motion to a standstill.

The forest was populated with leafless trees and the night was gloomy as darkness surrounded us, like that of a blanket on a cold winter's night. The air was once again thick, porridge-like; the kind of porridge you hated as a child and never wanted. I widened my eyes in search for clarity. The length of the road could be seen in the distance as the cabs light shows, and it seemed we may have disturbed what lurks at night as eyes started to open behind the trees. There was blood everywhere, the driver had been thrown out and was on the ground lying still - maybe dead or just hanging onto his dear life. I had noticed earlier that he wasn't wearing his seatbelt. I got out of the cab and wondered whether I should move Nicole or not and so I left her untouched. There was a big hole in the side of her stomach and blood poured out from where my child was sleeping. She moved as I held on to her - her grip on my arm was weak but it was present.

"Everything is going to be ok." I told her. "You'll be fine." I took my phone out of my pocket and to my utter shock it was still in one piece. I called the ambulance; twenty minutes they said.

"I don't want to die," she sobbed. "I want to give birth to our child," she continued as her hand that was now filled with blood caressed and rubbed her stomach. She cried even harder.

"I'm sorry, this is not how I planned it baby," I whispered into her ears as I kissed her whilst holding her head with one hand and my other hand trying to stop the blood from oozing out of her side. I pressed my hand against the wound as if it would push life back into her body. I was desperate and I had to try something. I panicked as the weight of her body pressed against my sore wrist; she was slowly slipping away. I looked up and around for the ambulance that claimed to be twenty minutes away. Her body was starting to get limp and cold. The sound of the sirens caused my ears to perk up.

"They are almost here baby, hang in there, please, I beg you!" I said to her and just like that I cried out, looking for help once more.

"Please!" I shouted in the darkness of the night; we were in the middle of nowhere. Then I heard a weak voice coming from the driver on the ground as he moaned and groaned, still unable to move from his deathbed. I looked up frantically at the blue lights. I could see them flashing but they seemed far away and the only person that meant the world to me was slowly slipping away from me, fading away like saw-dust blows away in the wind. Without her I was going to be lonely, afraid and unwanted.

"I'm sorry, I'm sorry I allowed this to happen," I told her. A voice interrupted my last moments with her and in a deep cinematic tone said: "I'm in charge now, this was always going to happen; from the day you betrayed me, this was going to happen." I was like a puppy and he was a big dog and there was nothing I could have done - no words were to leave my mouth, no words could have explained the feelings felt at that moment, so I didn't try. I cried out again and this time words formulated; the heavens were the destination or, maybe the hells, any-one that would replace her pain for mine, no one in particular, just to whomever would accept my plea and answer the cry.

Nicole tugged on my shirt to calm, drew me closer and, whispered, "I know what my sister did to you; I spoke to her yesterday and she told me what you did. All along I have known what happened."

I gasped in disbelief and shock and at that moment I contemplated dropping her right there and leaving her for dead or perhaps pushing the branch in deeper into her side. The only thing that stopped me was the fact that my dead child was in the way. My eyes swelled up again; this time it was blood. I stood up, leaving her momentarily as my breath was taken away and so was my heart, twice - I could have died right beside her. I tried looking around for something to aid me but I couldn't find anything sharp. The voice spoke once more. "Get up and leave," he said, "she has betrayed us for too long; she should have told you she was against you the whole time – can't you see that?" he bellowed. The sound echoed in the night, causing the trees to shake.

"Leave me alone!" my defeated tone begged.

"What are you telling me?" I asked her directly. "What am I supposed to do with that information?" I grunted. No answer came from her mouth, forcing me to shout it out louder and louder, causing the stillness of the dark to shuffle in fright and eventually I received an answer. The ambulance was near and I could see them now.

"I always loved you," she said. "Despite everything my sister did, I still loved you. I don't know why I continued to be with you after she told me, but I did anyway. I couldn't turn my sister in: she was blood. I have no regrets and I will never stop loving you." Her words travelled in the distance of the long road, creating silence as it went, and my mind travelled after her last words, hoping to catch them in a jar of memories. I was too late. This was to be her legacy, I thought as I peered my eyes back at her noticing a single stroke of tear rolling down her cheek: life was gone; the last remaining strength in her neck had vanished leaving her head fall to the side of my arm and the warmth of her body departed, taking her soul with it. I held her tight once more, then released. The ambulance had arrived.

CHAPTER 12

The sound of moans and groans coming from a distance pierced through the thin sheets separating the patients, it sounded as if a pig was being slaughtered. It was high pitched and stung like an arrow entering flesh.

"It's only Henry," a faint smoking voice whispered. The voice was only meters away from me and since the curtains were within reach, I reached out and parted them, exposing the face of a man who looked like worms had been eating him from inside out or a man severely malnourished. He opened his mouth, and it sounded like only dust came out; there certainly wasn't any sound. He coughed out the last cigarette he had not long finished. It was chesty like when a hammer beating a stubborn nail, the presence of the cigarette was oblivious as the smell was still strangling the freshness of the air. The moans and groans were no longer there and instead it had turned into screaming. Was he being operated on? I wasn't sure, but all I knew was he was in too much pain and it wasn't going away. The screams were too much and I couldn't go back to sleep, as much as my body needed it - my heart, head and soul needed to rest even more. Tears started to well up in my eyes; they knocked and knocked but there was no answer, I wasn't able to cry. I couldn't do it any more. Nicole was gone. I turned my head away from the man next to me because I didn't want him to see my pain.

I didn't know whether to love her or hate her and so I choose both.

I was shattered into pieces, my emotions were scattered like a nation of ants and it seemed putting me back together was impossible. I was losing my mind and wished the accident had taken me as well. I now faced loneliness in a hospital bed and my worst nightmare had come true. The woman of my dreams was no longer a part of the dream but instead was now a thing of the past. My mind drifted towards her sister, and the rest of them.

"I am going to kill them!" I whispered to myself.

"Kill who?" the smoker's voice asked, not realising that I had actually said it out loud.

"Myself," I replied, hiding my true intentions from the ever-listening ears of this man. I needed to get out of here: I mulled for a while looking around for an escape route as the voices in my head had taken over. The pain in my head began to pulsate even more as I thought of Nicole. I had mapped out the route for my get away; this place wasn't for me. I discharged myself and went to the nearest bus stop. My good friend Rob would be glad to see me, I thought to myself before trying to get up. The first attempt failed, the shock in my head and the pain in my body was enough to sit a grown man down - it felt like electric shock had cut through my flesh. The second attempt was a success and I was up and running, as fast as a wounded solider could.

"No kind of help will get you through this," the voice said, pushing through a crowd of my thoughts to tell me I'm worthless.

"Your decisions brought you here but what you were asking to do was just impossible." "I wasn't ready to take someone's life," I tried to negotiate with him, but he wasn't going to budge. I was next and consequently doomed, there was only one way it was going to end. I searched for my phone, the only thing that survived the crash. I called Rob but there was no answer; I got sent straight to voice mail, with the voice note that came after the beep suggesting that he had gone abroad.

We had planned a trip that was supposed to happen in a few days but that definitely wasn't going to happen.

I moved in the direction of his house, my clothes full of blood stains but to me there was no amount of shame that could amount to the pain that I was going through and so I continued without a care in the world. I knocked on the door but there was no answer, I decided to peep through the window for search of any activity but he was gone. I sat outside the house for a while, swinging my feet mid-air. The voice in my head was laughing, the laugh was sarcastic, purposeful and mean.

"You stupid fool," he said. "You idiot, everything that has happened has been your fault. Your parent's death, your wife's death, you killed them all; it is all your fault and you should just do yourself a favour and kill yourself," he concluded the tirade of abuse. "Your life has no meaning now, no one will miss you, much less notice you have gone. You think Rob actually cares about you?" he jeered.

"Yes he does," I jumped in.

"Do us all a favour," he took back control, "Just die!" he shouted. "Remember that bridge you passed to get here?" he pointed directing my gaze to the bridge that runs on top of a busy junction. It was massive and was clear to see, even from Rob's house, "Go and jump from the top, head first, it will be quick and painless." It felt like he gave me a cheeky wink as a means to a full stop, so I didn't say anything in return. The anger in his tone meant he was serious, and every word that came out was meant to cut deep. I got up and looked at the window of Robs house, revealing my reflection. Thoughts of justice slithered through my ears.

"You're right," it said, "maybe dying was the only way out and then maybe all my pain would go away." I left the house, walked towards nowhere in particular, and half way down the highway I realised I was walking home. I remembered a bar that wasn't too far from home, so I changed course, walked past the bridge - ignoring the fact that at any moment a gust of wind could have blown me into the road.

"Careful now, Andreas," the voice said casually, "I'm not done having fun with you; I don't want you to depart just yet," he mocked.

The bar was full; that was evident by the amount of drinkers outside on the deck chairs. The bar was ideally located on the side of a roundabout and the name on the swinging sign read 'Happy Hat'. My long legs had taken me all this way. I looked at my watch and it read nineteen forty-five. The building had flowers hanging from the side of the it, orange lilies, tulips, sun flowers and the likes and they trailed around the wall like a well decorated tree. I was on the other side of the road looking in as cars passed in a hurry causing me to take a few steps back. The voice in my head had other ideas tugging at my feet and prompting them to take just a few more steps towards destiny; not the bar but the death that had been following me ever since I was born. The voice controlled my mind and he was now in charge of my body.

"Walk," he said, "just a few more," he continued. A car sped past me blowing its horn and the driver shouted all manner of profanities at me as I watched helplessly. I was an empty shell, there was no sign of a human being, I was tired. My wounds were still fresh and had I been a dog I would have been licking them by now. The pain in my side was evident, my ribs had been broken narrowly missing my lungs, the pain was still there and it made me wince every time I moved. Even as I lay on the hospital bed it would occasionally go away and come back and it felt like someone had punched a hole through my side with a knife. It was that bad, even as I pushed the bar door open I was almost tumbled to the floor. I had to hold myself up on the gold door knob, took a seat and ordered the strongest drink they had, vodka. The lady behind the bar was a short, five feet something, dark haired lesbian. If she wasn't I would be surprised but I was almost pretty sure she was. I know I was judging her but I couldn't help it. She had a nicer hair cut than I did and I also noticed bruises around her eyes, kind of like she was being abused. I chose to stay out of it and so I never asked. I wanted to but I refrained myself from doing so. I got the drink and took a seat, taking slow sips and I could feel it slip through my blood stream providing relief from the pain. It was a nice warm feeling making me want more. I took another shot, and another and it made me feel good since it was taking away my worries in the process but unfortunately I couldn't get what happened last night out of my head. The voice spoke but his words staggered, so he repeated it, this time slower, making sure each word was heard,

"The man across from the room has been watching you for the last half hour," it said.

"Where?" I asked, entertaining the temptation. I wasn't able to think logically, so he took advantage of my weakness and made me walk over to the overly large man. His head was bald and his beard was huge; he looked scary. He reminded me of a bully from college, except this one was a lot bigger. I looked him dead in the face.

"Whatchu looking at?" I shouted. My words were minced; even I could tell, but my tongue was not corresponding with my intellect. I was speaking gibberish and I could tell he didn't understand what I was saying, undoubtedly causing him to hammer my right shoulder with a mighty fist. The force of the blow caused me to take several steps backwards, maybe ten or so. I was so far away from him at that point I should have gone home. I didn't want to fight him after that and so he continued to enjoy his drink, leaving me to stagger back to my seat.

"You ok there, pal?" the bartender asked. "What pain are you trying to get rid of, mate?" she continued to ask. The alcohol numbed my senses causing my tongue to be heavy and so I didn't respond. I staggered to my feet with the little strength I had, knocked a smaller man's drink almost to the ground. He wasn't scared of my size which was because of the embarrassment I had put myself through earlier.

"Sorry," I mumbled without making eye contact and made my way to the bathroom, almost falling flat on my face once more. I walked with my arms stretched out in front as a guide dog leads the blind, my eyes blurred and fuzzed - took my limp meat and pissed all over the floor. I smiled, completely missing the cubical; the drink gave me a sense of confidence for a brief moment forcing me to make a mess on the floor and went to order one last drink before I walked out of the bar. At least there was little sense left in my head enough to remember the direction home and it didn't take long before I was home. I reached the front door with the key already in my hand, tried to fit it in the slot but it wasn't cooperating. The weight on my legs gave in and I fell with a big thud on the floor and immediately passed out with my head leaning against the door. I was barely conscious, my eyes half way open but thankfully I was aware of what was going on. The old man from next door came out and helped me through the door and onto the bed then left without a trace.

CHAPTER 13

The night had gone and the morning had arrived, I woke up with the sound of drums playing in my head. No sound was playing, just the thumping feeling of someone standing on my head and beating it like a bongo drum. The regrets from last night was reeling off my tongue and my head was too heavy to lift and so I continued to lay in bed until the weight had eased.

It was a few hours after I had unsuccessfully tried to get up but the second attempt was a success as I rolled to my side of the bed, planting one feet at a time. The shower was my next mission and a cold one at that, considering that the night had been baking hot and the bed was wet, not from the bile of my stomach but just pure sweat. I wasn't sure how to take Nicole's death. I saw her face all around the flat and wanted to smash every photo she had been in. The bad taste in my mouth was ever present and I only noticed it when I saw her face. "How could she have done this to me?" Though feeling distraught and betrayed, my body revealed the red blood cells from the strength I was using to scrub the guilt from my heart scrubbing harder it began to hurt. My nails was once again in my arm, it was becoming a common thing and this time drawing blood in the process as I watched it slither down the drain like a snake escaping from a predator. I continued to blame myself - though it wasn't anything new - but I kept on thinking it. I stepped out the shower before I had fully soaked with the skin on my fingers wrinkled and whiten like the feeling you get when you know you have been in water far too long. I got dressed as quick as I could, walked in the living room and was met by the large mirror right on cue to create disaster. "Punch it," he said. "Punch it as hard as you can." Before I could process the command my left hand, the weakest, was heading through the glass. Smash! It connected leaving millions of pieces on the floor. My thoughts raced themselves into a maddening tangle as I thought about going for a fly with the birds outside. Something was stopping me from taking my life which was holding me back. It was like if I was able to conjure up the courage or the gut-less emotion of fear and I would be able to be free. *Was that the formula to set myself free?* I wonder. The thought quickly left my mind as I saw a picture of me and Nicole. It looked like we were in love. "Punch that one too. She betrayed us and I'm glad she's dead," He said lowering his tone as he ended. "shut up," I blazed. "You know I'm right," he continued ignoring my command as if I was rankled. "They all need to die now." I heard the comment as much as I didn't want to hear it. I heard it and it tasted good. I wanted it and needed redemption. I looked in one of the millions of pieces on the floor and saw red in my eyes.

A knock on the door. The image I saw when I peeped through the peep hole was that of the old man. I opened the door and walked away, giving him an inviting gesture to come in. I needed to reconnect and he was offering. The old man followed me in, asking if I was ok. "Yes I'm fine," I replied. It sounded rude as it left my lips but I was able to catch it before it had reached its destination. I fired back a question at him, causing him to rethink the next words. "Thank you for helping me last night, I really appreciate it." "That's ok young man," he fatherly uttered. "Are you sure you're ok?" he investigated further. I paused for a moment, a very brief moment, shook my head and made sure he understood by saying, "No."

"Don't tell him anything," the tormentor abruptly shouted. "Don't tell him a word you fool, he doesn't need to know anything about us. Some people just want to know your business and laugh at you." My eyes rolled up and stayed there as if I was searching for the rodent in my head. I wanted to see if he was sweating. The panic in his eyes and the dry stains at the side of his mouth sounded like fear, which was something I hardly saw. There was a level of permanence in his heart beat as if he feared the old man. My eyes levelled out and found the gaze of the old mans eye balls and began to explain to him what went down last night. Just as I did with the doctor, I left out no details.

The old man took his attention away from the heavens outside and maybe he once flew with the bird of the sky. I wondered as I watched him as his gaze somewhat suggested a familiarity in them. His eyes moved and met mine and there was a thin moment of silence; as if we were collecting our thoughts through the pits of a trash can. He opened his mouth and it was like I could see each word as they exited. "Listen, young man," he said. "All of what you have just said I have been through and this was my life at one stage. I know your pain and I felt what you have felt before. I'm sad to say this, but sometimes it doesn't end well. I'm here now but what I have lost was everything to me. My life was ruined by the voice as he wasn't only in my head but walked beside me. Everything I felt was real and the pain was unbearable." I looked at him while he shook his head, as it seemed as though the memory was still raw although it was so long ago.

"I could see that the crust of the scar was not fully healed. This should not be taken lightly," he said as his voice escalated to the level of a teacher. "This should not be taken lightly," he expressed as he held the decibel to maximum level. "Let's get out of these four walls," he said. "Let's go for a walk and I will tell you some more of my story." We stepped off the warm flat. There was hardly any breeze blowing to relieve the sweat from my arm pits and the one-eyed dog was waiting on the other side of the door. He laid there as if he was guarding the place and was slow to get up. *Not much of a protector, are you*? I thought. He walked with us down the road. The old man and I walked side by side as I glanced over my shoulder to the image of the dog wobbling like a penguin to create a forward motion. I wondered if he had been with the old man since birth and wondered what his story was. On the outside it looked like I was coping well and looked like I was social and fun but on the inside I wanted to be alone or with a very few. "I feel uncalled to act or perform. The world and I are very opposite," I sighed involuntarily and of course apart from the bruises I was ok. I had to be, and was never going to let the voice win.

The old man paused, stitched his brows together and opened his mouth to say something, then stopped. It was like whatever he was going to say he mid way thought against it. A few moments of silence filled our steps as we continued to walk. "I'm from a place called Jinja," he began again, "which is located at the edge of Lake Victoria. We speak a language called Lusoga and majority of us are of the Bantu people." I felt like I was in a lecture back in college days and the lecturer went on and on. "My home is Uganda," he expressed with a sight that expressed a sense of returning. "I've traveled far and near back in my day and I've come a long way, certainly a long way from home now. I met my wife back in our village and had nothing compared to western worlds - but we had everything we needed. She was the most beautiful girl I had ever seen and I was around 15 while she was 13. I asked around of who she was and the first time I saw her, I didn't see her again for a long time; but her face was printed in my brain and every now and again that image would flash up. I continued to ask around but to no joy. It was like she had disappeared or I had imagined her as that's what many of my friends told me, but I was sure she was real. It was like two energies crossing paths and a segment would always be left for reference. Eventually after five years, I saw her again at a big wedding in our community. My eyes locked on her and hers locked on mine as we approached each other like a conveyer belt pulling us together. We danced, spoke and was instantly connected and she was to never leave my side from that night onwards. One year later we got married and nine months later our son was born. It was magic prior to meeting my wife. My past was very troubled as I had done many bad things. Things I am not pleased with."

I took my eyes away from the path I was walking and placed it onto him. He looked pale; as pale as a dark-skinned man could get, and it seemed as though his past memories came with a sense of haunting. I broke the awkward gaze and placed it back in the direction I was walking. "I started hearing voices from the moment my wife gave birth, and it was like she gave birth to darkness or like a puff of dark cloud came out of her along with the flesh of my son. I was to ignore the voices until he was about five, which was when things took a turn for the worst. My father was a military man," he continued as we reached a coffee shop. "He was one of the most savage of killers and was ranked as one of the best. Hundreds of kills - man, woman and child - and there was no discrimination to his killings. There was one time he took me out with him and it was the arrest of a man that was on the wanted list. They dragged the man outside and shot him in his head in front of his wife and children. He screamed for his life while my father and his crew laughed. I looked at the child who was no older than I was but his fortune was not that of mine as I was on the other end of the gun while his father stared down the barrel of my father's rifle. Blood splattered, landing on the nail of one of my toes and I stared down at it without wiping it away. I was scared and the image has never left me ever since and has kept me up at night every now and again. That was just one of many trips I went along with my father and I believe that the voice has been related to these instances. The voices became one after a while, as the one seemed to have combined with all the others and tormented me for the rest of my life until I gained control."

My eyes perked up. "Control," I uttered. "You mean to tell me you won?" My voice escalated as the thought of control excited me. The old man nodded, "You first have to lose everything and everyone - it will bring you to the edge just as you are about to jump. Show no fear, then jump." I stared out the window of the cafe a few times and then back at the old man. His face seemed to be back to normal and his colour was back. He carried on with his story as he opened his mouth in a slow motion kind of way. It was like he struggled to move his tongue. "The voice," he said, "tore my family apart and gave me an ultimatum; that I was to cure my past and make amends or else he would remove those that I loved, one by one."

I thought of Rob and feared the worst for him. My body became cold again as those were the words whispered in my ear. He said, looking deep in my eyes, through my eyes and down my spinal cord and landed in the midst of my soul. I felt what he said and I was not alone, I thought. We left the cafe and went back to our home. The lazy or perhaps almost dead dog followed as instructed. The old man opened his front door, walked halfway in and looked back at me. "Next time I will tell you what happened to my son; for now be careful."

CHAPTER 14

It was an unusually gloomy morning in the city of London as the weather lady on the T.V. mentioned signs of weather change. My mood matched the weather as I laid in bed without a desire to move, with my curtains drawn, darkening the room to pitch-black levels. I laid curled up like a cocoon untroubled, un-bothered and unmoved as I stared at the light bulb in the ceiling, trying to see whether I could turn it on with just my thought. I had remembered a video I watched a while ago depicting the use of the other percentage of brain power. It didn't work. Maybe the sight of Nicole walking into the room to disturb me would light a spark in me again. Neither happened as my brown eyes shifted towards a crack in the wall and my eyes narrowed in, almost wishing it away. I remembered a quote I once read about a Japanese tradition. When a vase is broken, they would use molten gold to seal it back together and said it was better to mend something than to just simply buy a new one. The fact that it was mended would make it stronger, giving it a new lease of life and making it more sturdy. Thanks to its scars, it gave me faith along with the words of the old man.

My hand moved in a delicate slide to where Nicole once slept. It was not warm but cold in fact, calm and unused. I should be hating her but I can't; instead all the hate I have for her had been stored up for her sister. I was just waiting for the right moment to unleash it. I sighed an exhausted outburst of air, then the voice appeared and intervened. He spoke, "You are not strong enough and you are broken to the point of no repair. What you didn't read was that when the Japanese break a vase into a million pieces they throw it away. You've reached a million pieces and you'll soon be cast away in the dust bin," then vanished before I could get a chance to tell him he was wrong. Every single one of my thoughts were scrutinised like an FBI investigation, then would be sledge-hammered back down to the ground. I was not free in the sense of speech but the sound echoed in my dome and I was reminded who was in charge. I wondered why he didn't appear when I was talking to the old man. It furthermore added to the notion that he was afraid, afraid of what I thought and I was a defeated teacher that once had my life together, planned and was active. I dug my nails deep into my left arm and dragged it up to my elbow, exposing the white of the flesh that shed no blood. That was after I found myself stiffening in bed. I bowled my fist and in a frantic burst of adrenaline began to sprawl myself in a fighting motion on the bed, fisting and kicking. "Leave me alone," I whispered, soft and helpless. I knew he wasn't going to, but that's all I found myself saying over and over again. This was a constant remedy to ease the pain and anxiety. The pain of my nails digging deep into into my soft flesh took my mind away from the trauma, the loss and brings new pain that I can now control. My stomach rumbled, to which I paid no attention to as I tossed some more on the bed, falling off in the process and knocking my knee on the way down on one of the drawer handles. I got up with a slight hobble in my movement. The voice made a chuckle and sounded as if he was seated around a small table with only one chair present in the far corner of a room and a glass cup in his hand. I wasn't sure whether it was water or just empty. I could make out the hint of icy blue in his eye and the pale alabaster figure with a pointy nose. The chuckle sounded in a distance not far but not close. I checked my phone while climbing back up to my feet only to be alerted that today was the funeral. I felt nothing. Did I want to go? No! Did I go? I did.

The taxi pulled up to the church. I stepped out and was greeted by a beautiful stoned building which reminded me of the type of church Nicole wanted to get married in. There were times while we were on our many walks that she would just stop by a church she liked and looked at it. Sometimes when she was feeling her strange self she would walk up to it and stroke it. I brought my head back down from the peak of the building. The service had already started as the choir was singing. I had stayed away from her family for fear of, well, them knowing my past. I didn't want to been seen as I entered the church or interact with anyone for that matter. I snuck in and took a seat at the very back. I wore a black suit with a yellow tie which represented Nicole as her personality was filled with joy and cheerfulness. The black was the hate I had for her. I was also disguised with dark sun glasses to complete the lack of desire to be seen.

The service went on and people got up to say their goodbyes. They walked up to the coffin with tears in their eyes, enough to fill the church like a pool. They walked up as if they feared death and not a single soul was seated as I looked around, except me. I was still hidden out of sight. The words that laid on the ears of the congregation was that of admiration for her as they loved her and she went too early. "They never knew her," I thought shuffling in my seat, causing an unknown face to me to turn around. I ducked down. Further, they didn't know her like I did and I wanted to get up and say something, but the voice once again told me to stay seated. I wanted to tell them all to get out and wanted to tell them of the things the sister did to me. I wanted to do bad things but listened and kept my ass on the bench. "If you get up there, people will curse you down," the voice said. This time his voice was soft as if he cared about me. "They would blame you for her death. Why do you think they have been calling you? You are not missed, Andreas. They just want your head on a spike, " he threw out without consideration of what may happen. He continued to belittle me as I got up from my seat with my bum tingling with no sense of feeling, stormed out the church, slamming the door shut behind me with fury and the sound of a mass of people turning around to look in the direction of the door. I left the scene as quick as I could, not far but far enough to get away from the lies being told in the church. I wondered if Nicole's sister had heard about her untimely death and was curious if she was in the church. Whether she would be brave enough once again to show her face, I wondered adventurously. I didn't own a gun but I would find one.

Later that afternoon once she was six feet under. I visited the place where she took her final rest and stood over the freshly dug up patch; the smell the dirt and the cement where she laid was still fresh in the air. I bent my knees on my way down to say the final farewell, my eyes staring as a drop landed on the flowers left by loved ones – the rain caused it as it fell past my head. Lightening struck and the flood gates of the clouds opened and showered me with tears collected by the Gods. I didn't move as it would be the one and only time I would be in this place; I needed it to be time well spent. My suit soaked as it collected enough water to water a garden; it was a monsoon, the yellow tie shone bright amid of all the dark clouds, taking the place of the sun maybe; it glowed bright as if her spirit was outshining the darkness that evening. I rose to my feet and took one last check at the name on the tomb stone just to make sure it was hers, turned my back and walked off into the distance.

The journey home was a long one; I was soaking wet and every cab refused my presence and the bus was the only option. I didn't mind, I was used to it now. "You look a bit wet," the voice said, "you are going to get sick," he joked as the bus took a sharp turn, causing me to slide along the seat and lose my composure. The journey took me a solid forty-five minutes but it wasn't long before I was outside my door, searching for the keys before deciding to check if the old man was at home. I hesitantly knocked on the door; I didn't want to seem like I was bothering him. There was no answer as I began to walk away, but before I could reach inside my house the old man had opened his door - it must have been his age why he moved so slow to answer the knock. He invited me in, I entered the house and was slapped in the face with a surprise; the old man lived like he didn't have anything, no money, no possessions. I was shocked, widening my eyes like the lenses of a camera that scanned the room - there was no furniture anywhere. I continued to snoop, my pupils tightened in to focus, just to make sure I was not missing a trick, except there was no trick, this was the mystery all along behind door number eight, I thought with a satisfied look on my face. I didn't want to question his choice of living but I was sure my face asked the question, and right on cue the old man looked at me and asked, "Are you surprised?" to which I smiled, and replied a respected no. The fragrance of well-done sage and other herbs greeted me; I know it was sage as I remember the smell from Nicole's mother's house, she would always burn herbs - ward off evil spirits, she used to say. Incense welcomed me, it didn't smell bad, I thought.

"Take a seat," he said, and the command was direct and gave no choice.

"Where?" I asked in the most polite way possible, and trying not to sound rude I cleared my throat and lowered my voice as I retried the question. There was silence once more.

I whispered, "there is no where to sit." Still confused, I checked the ears of the old man to see if he was wearing a hearing aid; there was none, of course not, as I was with him yesterday and he was hearing fine.

"On one of the cushions on the floor," he broke the silence in the air. The look on my face was perplexed, uninterested and showed the need to rebel, but I showed respect and obeyed the request. There were cushions laid on the floor, two to be exact, and this reminded me of old Japanese movies I used to watch.

"The funeral was today," I announced as he took his seat opposite me. I wore a yellow tie to represent her living flame, and he had his fingers intertwined, watching me as each word flowed out my mouth.

He intervened and said, "life has its ways of building our muscles for us, making us stronger, tougher; it knocks us around until we are down, but the moment we decide to stand back up is the moment we become superheroes, this is the lesson you must take from this," he concluded.

"Don't listen to him," the voice said in a timidity tone - the shout almost burst my ear drums. I used my index finger to check to see if I was bleeding, to see if my brains were minced up and leaking out, but the old man continued the story of how he lost his wife

"She was the most beautiful thing that ever happened to me," he explained, "not only her looks but her mind was more attractive." I looked deep into his eyes and I instantly believed him; the look in his eyes showed the state of his heart, and it seemed clean, the passion in his eyes was warm. "She loved like no other and was willing to sacrifice at the drop of a hat," he said as if he knew that for certain, "life became easy once she was around, she always smelt of lavender, like she rolled around in it before she entered my presence." I sat there thinking of Nicole's love; it was a change to be out of the presence of all the pictures on the wall reminding me of her, instead I was surrounded by the blankness of a wall filled with nothing.

"The way Nicole loved me was the same," I uttered, but not wanting to interrupt the story I said no more, but all the memories flashed past my eyes as if it was a roll of film; while he spoke, in that moment I could smell her, remembering the last time I tasted her lips.

"Coconut," I whispered as a deaf tone left my lips, and tuning back to the old man's story.

"I hear my neighbours coming up the stairs, keys jingling, then doors closing," the old man continued, going on to say that the life he lived was made simple by this woman. I listened intently as I tried to refocus my attention.

"Her name was Grace," he pointed out with a smile.

"Fitting," I said, trying to add value to the conversation.

The wise man smiled and continued, picked up where he had left off and said: "In life we have to make decisions; sometimes the decisions you make will hurt at first but it will be best for the overall story of your life," he stated with some regret in his tone. He kept on looking away while telling the story, and I narrowed my eyes as if to question his actions. "She died," he mentioned, saying it with a subtle quiver of the lips, as faint as a whisper, as if he wanted to tell me the pain but held back in doing so, cutting into my wondering thought. He continued on with his story and in the process brought up the decision again.

"The decision that had to be made," he spoke, "was wether to live or for me and my whole family to die." He paused. "She wanted us to live," with an escalated voice as his big brown eyes scrutinised me - he was convincing. I was backed into a corner with nowhere to go but believe him. I slowed my heart rate down as my jaw dropped at the sound of her fate.

"She sacrificed herself," he apologised, not to me, but to her; it was like she could hear him. His fingers slipped from its once tight connection as he lost his composure.

"We were on a boat," he went on. "The boat rocked and swerved, like we were on the drunkenness of the belly of the deep blue sea. The waves collided with the small boat, knocking a few people out and over board but we didn't even look back and it was every man for themselves. We had to hold on, we had to be careful. We paid extortionate amount of money and it wasn't first class seats; as long as we made it to safety, none of that mattered, the pursuit was hot and we were in line of enemy sight. My wife fell out into the open waters. With all my might I made the driver stop and wait for her; I took his gun away from him and pointed it between the centre of his eyes. Time was running out and the driver wanted to leave, but it was a matter of life or death because she was in the water struggling to make it back to the boat. In all the commotion the gun was taken back from me but I wasn't interested in struggling for it as I was more concerned with my wife in the water. Our son was seated, secured and stayed still. The driver held on to the throttle and was ready to go, but I stopped him and stared straight into his eyes, and that stare told him I meant business and was willing to die so that she got back into the boat. She screamed out for us to go as the enemy was not far behind us. She knew if we had waited for much longer that all of us would be dead and that the enemy would show no mercy; they were people after my father, revenge they wanted, and their mission was that no one from the same blood was to be left standing. I was his son and he was already dead and wasn't able to protect me. All his bad deeds had finally caught up with him. She screamed out again, *"Go!"* this time the word was dragged out, echoing across the river.

"Go! Go!" she shouted as her lungs filled up with water.

"I love you," she mumbled. The river swallowed up her spirit and left her for the judgement of the underworld. I listened." He sighed. I wasn't able to maintain eye contact with him. It was too hard not to feel sorry for him, empathy filled my stomach but I was able to catch a glimpse of him as his head turned and looked at a small picture of her hanging on the wall, which depicted her in a small dress, smaller than a wedding dress but was still beautiful.

"Take care of my son!" she shouted. Those were her final words as the boat drove off. Minutes later, the sound of screams was heard in the not far distance and gun shots followed as the sound of scatters rang like rain on a zinc sheet."

I watched the old man. His fingers were interlaced again. His eyes closed; he didn't look like the crying type so I didn't expect it, but the memory that seemed like an old scab was lifted and exposed the redness of the wound.

"The water graced our company for hours," he moaned. "Maybe days, I wasn't sure. The boat had run out of fuel so we were just floating like a wonderer, my son was in my arms, cold and sick with pneumonia, and he was dying in my arms. The boat rocked to the rhythm of the waves, as if to put us all to sleep..." There was a loud car alarm going off outside as it interrupted the conversation, and it was welcomed as the intensity of his story boiled and became too much to contain. The alarm stopped and he continued by saying that his son died a few hours later. His head dropped and revealed my theory to be false - he had two streaks of tears that rolled down his eyes. The disappointment trapped him as he tried to move but all he could do was sway his head from side to side.

"The boat had reached its destination with only a few of us left to tell the tale. By the time my feet had touched land everything was lost; I had nothing more to fight for. Living was not a necessity any more and at that point the voice in my head had torn me apart. It convinced me that it was all my fault just like it does to you, that I should jump back in the water and never to come back up. I finally found a breakthrough when I discovered an ancient meditation technique called ***the alignment of the Chakras;*** the art of controlling the mind, body and spirit, allowing energy to flow through the spinal cord and I became a man again. I was able to forgive my father, he was my pain and my security all at the same time, in doing so I was able to make peace and live again. With a second chance at life to pursue the many happiness that life had to offer me, I moved to London in the early 2000's to set up my life, away from all the violence and troubles. Meeting you was no accident," he explained. As if I had heard the thought rolling unconsciously through my head, I pondered my next words. As the voice joined our fellowship, he reminded me what was at stake.

"Remember who you are!" he jolted with an electric shock in the back of my neck. "You are in no shape to do anything about your situation." He taunted as if he was somewhat scared of the possibilities of me freeing myself.

"Rob," he said, springing me to life. "Take his name out of your mouth." I blurted out, now feeling comfortable in the presence of a new friend. The words echoed in my ears and fell silent as if he heard and got the message as the old man, now poised as a warrior, prepared his next strike.

"So what's your purpose now?" he quizzed. "What do you live for?" he simplified the question as if to give me a hint for not understanding.

The reply was simple as the mission had never changed, "Peace, happiness and a family."

The rain was still beating on the roof top and the streets were people-free. The sky was grey like the sun was afraid of the dark and it was nowhere to be seen. Typical British weather, I thought. "Quite fitting," I mentioned with a smirk; it was faint, hidden and secretive, almost as if someone was watching my every move, my every step, except there was nobody, nothing. It was the first time since the accident that my teeth were able to be seen beyond the thickness of my lips, as smiling was something of the past in the recent days.

CHAPTER 15

A few months had passed that were filled with emptiness. Across the road from where I lived was a well-presented Chinese restaurant. I mean it was splendid and we were in there at least three days out of the seven available to us, the smell would always slither its way up the tubes of the wall, then knock on my door, creep past un-noticed and into my nose, like a ninja in the night, begging to be visited. We were weak to it and would always lose, and maybe that would explain why the scale never changed its figures. We always had an excuse. By the time the thought had finished dancing around in my head my feet had found the pavement opposite the place. It was quiet, inviting even more to walk in. We always laughed at the name of the place. ***Fo'yu*** it read, as a smile accompanied me, because it gave me comfort knowing that a little piece of Nicole was still to be preserved. I would always enter the doors and my orders were read out to me. My name was on their system and I was one of their most loyal customers and if there was a customer of the month section on the wall, my picture would sure be up there.

"Chicken cho Mein?" the waiter behind the counter asked. Her accent was strong, and in all my time coming here I was never able to understand the woman as her tongue made me second guess what I knew. Asian sounding, fanciful and exuberant, with a little high pitch

in the end of each words. "With special fried rice," she concluded. The order was entered into the till without me opening my mouth except a wordless nod. Aware that I was one man down, the waitress asked, "Where have you been? I haven't seen you in a while."

My answer was short and sweet, "Been busy," I said in a lazy way.

If English was her first language she probably would think my response was rude and never talk to me again, but she just gave me one of those nods with a smile. Everywhere I went there was a bitter taste in my mouth. Everyone knew us together, like we were a pair of socks. I hastened for the exit, grabbing the bag from her hand in the process; the *thanks* was subtle.

The sun had disappeared that afternoon as I sat by the window watching the outside world, and a fresh blissful breeze blew, causing a shiver to run down my spine. Something strange had happened, a be-thankful melodious song sang, the lady's voice pierced the air and found its way to me. She was on her balcony wearing only a t-shirt and a pair of trousers. Wasn't she cold? I wondered. Her balcony was no more than a couple hundred meters away from me and though she was singing a song unknown to me I moved to the pulsating tempo. She was light in complexion, hair tied back and was wrapped in a head tie. With each note she took she closed her eyes and glided, but it wasn't clear who she was entertaining. Nonetheless, I sat there watching like a paid concert, and when she had finished I gave out a faint togetherness with my hands - a quiet one but it echoed in my head matching that of thousands clapping. My phone rang interrupting the opportunity to ask for an autograph, it was my friend Rob. My head dropped in disappointment, not because I didn't want to talk to him, but because I had paused to gather my thoughts, to take a moment away from the ringing phone. I angled my ear towards the window in hope of another song being prepared but none came. Then the phone stopped ringing. He was calling in regards to the trip I had missed. I didn't want the voice to hurt anyone else I loved - the only person left in this world I could trust with my life; the demon terrier was running my life at that stage. It made me distance myself from the one person I had left.

"You don't deserve a family," he would say.

"You are destined to be alone, lonely in this world with no one to depend on, no one to care for you," his voice was dead, emotionless once again and showed a careless attitude, there was a load of unpaid letters that came through the door.

It was red, meaning overdue payments. I was well behind with everything, I was wrapped up in my own world, and didn't care about anything else. All the wedding things were not paid for and I was now in debt. The voice would tell me to leave them alone, to put them to one side and forget them, and that is what I did. It felt like an axe crashed down on my chest and the wretched beast was there with both hands to prise the flesh open, causing more damage and pain. His words were like a samurai sword slashing a soft tissue, except the damage was being done in my head, my brain was taking the hit like a punching bag. The phone rang again and again, and yet again. Rob was relentless but I just couldn't bring myself to press the green button. I sighed at the thought of what Rob must have been thinking. I was lost mentally, drained physically - I was being pushed to my limits, and I wondered where it would take me. To the edge, or over the edge? I wasn't sure. A load of letters fell through my letter box and piled up at the foot of the door. I gave them a glance but nothing more.

A couple hours had passed by while I dozed off when the sound of a drill blasted in the left side of my ear. With each press of the trigger it got closer like it was coming through the front door. I rose to my feet almost pulling a muscle. It was coming from the front door, I proclaimed with my eyes still half shut. I took a few steps closer, grabbing the knife left on the kitchen counter in the process as the door hissed and opened. I lunged forward in an act of self-defence.

"Stop!" a loud strident voice penetrated the air as it bounced off my ear drums. "Stop!" he repeated as he revealed himself to be a man changing the lock on the door.

"What are you doing?" I asked him, perplexed and readying myself to throw a punch at him squarely in the nose. He took a moment and a few sharp breaths. "I'm here to change the locks on the door.

"I was ordered to do so by the owner of the property," he confessed.

I was shocked. A sharp pain entered my body as my feet became numb; I didn't know what to do as the reality I dreaded was happening. I was being kicked out of my home, a place I built and was proud to call home and I felt sick, helpless. Where was I to go? I wondered. Rob crossed my mind but only for a brief moment, and then left just as fast.

"Let me get a few things," I asked. He nodded and was relieved that I was no longer infuriated. I released the balled fist that was meant for battle. He noticed my defence was down and was more relaxed at the sight.

I walked away from him and packed as much things as I could in a small rucksack; It was hard but I had to do what was necessary. I was being kicked out and I had to own up to it.

"Besides, it is your fault." A faint voice mentioned, as if it was far away.

The house was in a state. Cleaning up was less a priority. Take away boxes were scattered all over the place. Clothes were left unwashed and to be honest I hadn't showered in days. The house stank. The mirror in the living room was murky. No image was able to reflect on it. The man at the door continued to drill. I needed to move out but I didn't want to go on these terms. Nicole would have been disappointed with me. I took all the pictures from the wall and placed them into a plastic box from under the bed. In my rucksack were things I needed for about a week then I would come back and get the rest. I placed valuable things in there just in case I had to sell for some cash. My accounts were in minus. I had nothing. The smell of blood entertained my nose for the next minute.

"Nicole," I whispered and closed my eyes in disbelief. The unpaid bills, the red letters that kept on dropping through the door, they all lead up to this moment. Trails of regret flowed through my mind as I walked over to the window and took one last look. The birds were not there but in all honesty I was trying to look past where they once danced. I turned my back, put my watch on, and left.

The night appeared out of nowhere as I looked for a place to rest my head. I had no place warm to go except the option of Rob's calling voice. He kept on calling. Perhaps he suspected something had gone wrong or perhaps someone had told him of Nicole's death. My tiring body wanted to go see him, to lay my head to rest but my mind was against it. Eventually, I would go see him but not that day. It wasn't the best idea, as I found out later, the frost was resting where it landed, creating a slippery surface.

"A single thought has more strength in effectiveness than a physical action," said the guy on the radio. The car continued past as the voice on the radio faded along with the sight of the tail light. Mental health was the topic. I continued to walk in the night. The temperature had dropped to below zero. I had enough clothes on but was still cold. I shivered as the sight of frost glazed the floor. I searched for a place to lay my head, a bench, I thought as I turned my head in search of a dark corner. I concluded admitting defeat, a defeat that would prove to be quite detrimental. I was a novice at being homeless, just the thought alone frightened me. My backpack was becoming heavy and I needed a place to rest it. A bench presented itself down an ally way. My intuition lit a light in my stomach and mentioned that it wasn't safe. I didn't listen, dropping the bag like it weighed a ton. The seat was wet as I travelled my hand over it causing a splash. I took a jumper out of my bag and laid it on the wooden seat, curled up into a ball, all the while trying to keep as warm as I possibly could. I felt degraded, worthless, just as the voice once told me. It was all coming true, I had to do everything I could to survive that night.

The sound of mutated rats accompanied me. They ran riot that night. A crack in the side of the building paved the front of their accommodation. One by one they stepped out as if they had done that every night. The noise was what woke me from what seemed as a thirty minute nap. Their little twitches and scratches rung to the core of my nervous system creating a sense of self destruction within me. It caused me to be anxious, scared and made my skin itch. The sound was like nails scraping a card board box trying to escape the torture of the heat, the smell was poisonous and blinding. It burned my nose like I had smelled the world's hottest pepper. My eyes watered as I sat up, now fully awake and unable to go back to sleep. The sheer toxicity of the rodents that resided among me was my punishment. I felt that the universe was giving me a life sentence. I wasn't to argue, I just accepted the ruling laid down on me. I was already on my knees and was unable to sink any lower. Pedestrians walked by without much of an acknowledgement. I felt sub-human more and more as the night went on, like layers of my skin were being stripped off from the foundation of my vessel piece by piece. My watch read midnight as the second hand made a final jump, footsteps paced their way towards me. The steps were heavy and meaningful. It sounded like whoever was prodding meant business. The stomping figure appeared as if he was a night watchman.

"You are new!" he shouted in the distance as he walked ever closer. His voice was sharp like that of an arrow. His figure in the distant reminded me of a pimp from Harlem.

"Are you deaf?" he shouted. His voice remained the same, as if he was trying to deepen it.

"You are new," he repeated, as if the location I was in was some sort of club I had to register to or at least formally introduce myself. I made eye contact with him. He was definitely not a pimp. His demeanour was scruffy like he lived on the streets also. He smelt like he came out of the same hole the rats lived in. Then I thought of how he would've fit through their door which was the crack. I closed my mouth as the thought ran past it without stopping to leave. I thought carefully about aggravating the situation, so I said nothing.

"I asked you a question," the sharp voice said, all the while scanning the possessions that laid beside me. There was nothing within touching distance from me. My watch was still on my hand. It was covered up all this while except when I stood up to welcome the unwanted guest. I saw his eyes locked onto my wrist as I slid my sleeve back over it. I knew something was about to go down. I was reading myself. After all I was at least twice his size and was not going down without a fight. My bag was on the bench as I stood forward. I made a move to get out of the situation and leave. I dropped my left shoulder, and without turning my whole body to pick up the rucksack on the bench,

'Smash!' was the sound I heard. I had heard the sound before I felt a warm liquid running down the side of my head, past my ear.

'Thump,' was the second sound that followed after. I saw the fist coming towards me but was unable to react, the glass bottle in the side of my head had dazed me. My feet said to go down but my brain hung in there. I kept on my feet. Conveniently, there was no one that walked by at that time. It seemed like he ran that street, like his goons were on each end as the look out. Pain plastered all over my face. My head was in a bad state, nothing registered at that time. I was out for the count as my body finally took a tumble and laid there in a heap of mess. I was a big man in size and I went down hard. It was a miracle that I didn't do any further damage. I finally connected the dots that the man was a mugger, a fate I concluded once I woke up and noticed that my bag was gone, my possessions were gone. It was stolen. I sighed. My fingers were now numb. I had never fully recovered from the cab accident and was still sore in some places, the grim reality developed in front of my eyes. All I wanted was the poem Nicole wrote for me. The side pocket! I thought as the images in my pupils took me to its exact location. I was changing, my once timid, shy and isolated frame was becoming a thing of the past. I got up instantly as if I was ordered by a sergeant. I exited the ally, slipping on the surface in the process. I marched down the main road in search of the villains, the thief. I had no idea where I was going, I didn't even see the direction he took. All I remembered was laying there looking up to the sky. The flakes that fell were many. Their whiteness was clear in the backdrop of the dark sky. I wanted to fight my fears, I needed a physical form to hit, punish, torture and most definitely kill.

I needed this. I desired it more than anything else. I was beginning to think I wanted it more than I wanted Nicole back. The voice was my Kryptonite. Every time he spoke, I would say how high, his voice was, like water being poured on the electrical system of my body. I continued to wander the streets that night. I hobbled, bumping into dust bins, time ticked on as it struck two in the morning, no sleep and with a bruised head. I was to give up, accepting another loss in the process, the adrenalin had worn out of me and the pain was kicking back in. I fixed my fingers to my head in search of blood. I remembered a cracking sound as the bottle collided with my skull. It felt as though it was cracked. What if my brain started leaking? I wondered as a panicked worry was painted all over my face. I found a seat to rest my legs, as I feared the fall that would inevitably come sooner or later. The voice appeared beside me, reminding me of who I was, and what I had done.

"You deserve to be out here," he said with a hint of arrogance in his tone.

"You are enjoying this, aren't you?" I asked as I felt the urge to irritate him.

"Get your ass up!" he shouted, causing my head to beat even faster with pain pulsating all over. "If only you had followed the instructions given and killed that witch, you would not have been in this situation, what do you have to say for yourself?" he asked.

Anger and fury was found in my voice as I shouted, "Why do you have to remind me of that all the time? Don't you think the feeling reminds me every day?" I continued to shout. It was a lucky thing it was late, or should I say early in the morning, because I would have been taken for a nut job or drunk and I was none of the above. I cared about what people thought of me. That was a thing of the past. Society didn't deserve what I had to offer, but that was me. I had to be stronger. In some ways the voice was right. I needed to be stronger, and guess he was teaching me a lesson. The blood from my entire body rushed to the peak of my head causing me to fall flat to the ground. My body was limp, unconscious and unresponsive. I laid there without a choice as the sun began to rise.

CHAPTER 16

The sound of sirens and moving vehicles captured the air around me and my thoughts were drowned out, silenced. It was like an alarm clock in the earliest part of the morning, and that alarm was followed by a stampede of footsteps. My eyes were still closed but my ears were awake. The fragrance in the air smelled sour, like my nose was on the floor of a drain as the water ran past it. I opened my eyes one lid at a time, while at the same time trying to get up from the pebble that had been digging at my side. The movement of my joints was shaky as they clunked as I rose, and I felt the tendon of my left knee jolt to one side as if to say that the pressure was too much. They were lifeless but I was able to use the bus stop to aid my attempt, and it felt like helping hands had stretched themselves out to my help. It was the same bus stop I had used that very night to shelter me from the bitter cold, and I slipped and slid as grip was not easy. "Thanks," I thought, grateful for the help. I had been knocked senseless, purely for trying to rest my head. My first night was difficult as I leaned by the stop thinking, I asked myself, "Am I able to do this another night?" My head dropped from its upright position. "No," I thought as the answer came to me in a hurry. I checked my pockets for my phone. I searched in a frantic panic as communication would be difficult. Not that I wanted to speak to anyone, as Nicole was the only one I wanted. She was constantly on my mind, and I still loved her despite her betrayal. When the one I relied on was gone, it was hard to know where I belonged, but I realised that I didn't belong to the streets. I needed to talk to someone; I had to, because the very loneliness I was running from was running very close behind me, chasing me, sometimes ahead of me. It had to stop. I was lost in an entrapment style fantasy that gave me no hope, a pawn-like status on the biggest chess board you could have imagined. I breathed a sigh of relief that could only be explained as one of finding breath from being under water for a long period of time. The tips of my fingers came in contact with my phone. I was ecstatic as my fingers wiggled into the hole of the pocket where it was hiding and saw thirty-seven missed calls and nineteen messages lit up in my face! Some from the landlord, others from the unpaid charges for the wedding preparations that never happened, I continued to scroll as a message from Rob read: ***Listen mate, I know you must be going through rough times. I heard about the death of Nicole and I want to say how sorry I am. Words can not explain how much pain you are currently going through. She helped you to be a better person. I knew you loved her by the way your eyes would light up whenever her name was mentioned. As I said before…*** I paused mid-sentence as I was interrupted by the pain in my side and I pressed my hand against it in the hope of suppressing it. ***I am always here for you***, I continued reading. ***So please allow me to help you, please call me back, and stay safe***. The message was concluded with a full stop. I wanted to read more, the words clothed me and hid my nakedness. I felt warm for that moment, I looked at my phone and read the message again. With each time I did, the warmth faded, revealing my shame, Rob was on my mind as I walked in the direction of the station.

"He knows about Nicole," I whispered under my breath, causing a hot mixture of air to dance with the cold sensation on my face. Every word that came out of my mouth fell to the ground like a snow ball as my lip trembled. Rob understood: I wondered if Rob understood what

I was going through as my eye ball rolled around its socket in search of a reason to believe otherwise. I needed him on my side. I realised I still had a few coins trapped in the hole of my pocket and I shook my trouser leg to identify the location of the jingles. The final shake saw the coins came rolling out of the bottom of the leg and rolled across the pavement, and I chased after them with only a few steps. It was however too late as they were collected by an open drain to be lost forever. I was beyond annoyed, my body was in pain, my movements were limited, something on the inside must be broken, I gathered. The phone was still in my palm, and I searched for Rob's number, hit the dial button and shakily put the phone on my ear, only to be told that I had insufficient funds to connect the call. I was disappointed as I dragged the phone away from my ear, pressing it against my face in a slow motion, then I remembered that my phone bills weren't being paid so the company must have cut it off. As if that was a surprise... Ha!

Of course they would! I thought.

"They are only interested in knocking someone when they are down," I growled as I rolled my fingers into a fist as though readying to hit something. This unconscious anger and rage was never apart of me, this constant need to hit something was becoming my release. I hated it and wanted to change, but the question was: do I have the strength? I had to scrap the plan as my wobbly legs took me past the train station and the bus stop. I was already exhausted but I continued to walk. Luxuries that were once taken for granted were no longer attainable at a snap of a finger or a click of a button. If only wishes were horses... I continued to walk almost forgetting the pounding headache that accompanied me wherever I went. It was like a fly that would not go away and could never die. I stopped outside a shop, leaned in without stepping through the door way and asked:

"Can I please have a bottle of water? I am very thirsty."

"No!" the shopkeeper replied. He spoke with finality as though to suggest that he didn't give the idea of helping a second thought.

I realised I was becoming a beggar so I walked on. I swallowed the saliva I could conjure up to quench my thirst and continued to walk.

The walk to Rob's house was tedious and the terrain was unforgiving, causing sores on my feet as hills and valleys presented themselves along the way. Slight exaggeration but there might as well have been, I dragged my feet as the weight became like an anchor, the faces of people in better positions watched as I walked past them. A smell emitted from my lacklustre body tasted like fermented fruit - a cloud filled with bad smell that would occasionally burst and I would be reminded of it as it followed me like a dark cloud. I frowned and rubbed my nose trying distinctively to brush it off. I understood their reactions but not their judgements. There was always a level of misunderstanding when you live in a place like this. The pace was fast and relentless and one had to keep up lest you would have been swallowed up, like a snake does his prey. I continued to walk past all the incredulous eyes peering at me without shame, but I paid them no attention and blocked their judgemental gaze out of the door of my sensitivity. The evolution of walking would be skates, that was my thought as I watched the rush, the fast walks and more often than not the runs from people trying to get about their business. It was a never-ending treadmill.

"They all need skates," I thought, sliding around like a performer of the ice. You would occasionally catch a glimpse of someone causing a scene, looking for attention, their lucky break of fame and many times they would be lucky as the sheepish culture of this society would acknowledge the stupidity and create a celebrity out of dirt. I snapped out of the horrid fantasy I had created and continued to walk - the journey to Rob's house wasn't far in distance, but the sheer thought of the walk crippled me before I had even started. My legs lost the oxygen they needed to operate a few times. It was a horrible walk considering the condition I was in; - my body was a complete wreck. Last night had knocked the last breath out of me. The November breeze blew and touched my spine, sending shivers through my whole body, and my nervous system was now weak. I begged for mercy but none was shown, I was running on an empty stomach - no food, no drink. The sheer fact that I was not going to accept defeat propelled me on; I was determined to recreate what I had, and the voice wasn't going to win. The three that abused me weren't going to win. I was torn between revenge and letting forgiveness. They were to pay a hefty price for the cardinal sin they had committed! My strides got smaller and smaller and I almost stumbled, but I managed to gather stability and reached the house.

"Knock, knock," was the sound the door made as I slammed the knocker uncontrollably. Rob peered through the peep hole as I noticed his large frame through the blurred glass, his wide hips and overly large stomach making him stand out. He door opened and we stood in the door way staring at each other, not knowing what to say, the silence between us was thick and needing carving before a word could penetrate. He looked at me with a mystified gaze, his eyes filled with shock, looking as though he wanted to trade places with me. Our bodies were still like a statue. For Rob to see me in such a state must have been terrifying for him; we grew up together, envisioned growing old together, still playing video games and laughing. The moment at the door seemed like ages. His stance changed, giving me the opportunity to ask:

"Aren't you going to invite me in?" His feet almost tangled as he moved out of the way, almost causing him to stumble. I managed to find the strength to firmly plant my feet in the front step of his house. My other leg was harder to lift as though it was rooted to the ground soaking up water from the earth. Rob grabbed my hand and helped me in, and as I grabbed his hand and felt a surge of energy transferred to me. For a moment I felt no more pain in my head. Rob's grip was that of love; It was firm and meaningful and we both embraced once the door was closed, just like a couple of long-lost friends would.

Rob placed his two hands on my shoulders; the weight of Rob's hands caused me to steady myself with an extension of my hand to the chair conveniently placed just beside me. With a sympathetic look and the narrowing of the eyebrows, he hugged me again, and this time a slight laughter came from my left ear and found itself seated at my right. The voice, I noted, he was laughing like he had a scheming plan.

"I hate you!" I whispered but Rob didn't hear.

The conversation between us was honest and painful. I told him all that had been going on, explaining the one event that pushed everything over the edge. The mood in the house was warm which made a change from the bitter cold of the outside. Rob's house was always clean and it smelt freshly done. This time we were seated in the living room instead of the fun room - there was no room for joking around. I apologised for going absent for the trip away, to which he said was okay. I sat in the chair and as comfy as it was, I was dying for a glass of water or anything really, just as long as it was a safe liquid to wet the linens of my insides. I gazed around the house as if it was the first time seeing it, or maybe a museum all the while Rob was still speaking, deaf ears were the destination his words found. I heard nothing from what he said in the last sixty seconds and was completely oblivious of the sound of his voice. All I heard was a flat-lined pitch that bounced off the many ornaments situated on various stands, and I used that time to muster up the courage to ask for that glass of water. I felt like a complete stranger in my oldest friend's house. I had often asked myself why and for the first time I realised that I knew exactly why. More strangely, I realised that I knew why all along; it was the very same reason why I didn't want to come here in the first place. I had a confused look on my face as Rob called my name, and it broke the flat line that had been playing. He must have been calling me for a while as the one I heard was loud and like a shout from down the road, except I was only two feet away from him. Nonetheless, he continued speaking. He was being his usual self, "Do you want ice with that?" he asked.

"No," I replied as he got up and walked to the kitchen. He was never the one to get emotional, cry or even show his feelings for long.

When we were in college, there was one instance where a girl he loved broke his heart. He called me that same hour and dragged me out of my house to go and celebrate. True, he wasn't happy about it, but he was more afraid of how it would make him feel if left alone to ponder. The following week I recalled seeing him in his room sloughed over his knees, sad, not crying but just sad. As soon as I stepped in he was back to normal, and it was at that moment I thought and came to realise that I had never seen him cry; he was like a rock, except he was weak for not doing so. He always bottled things up or masked them with jokes, and I always wondered how he did it while on the other hand I was quite the opposite. I took the water given to me and gulped it down in three.

"More please," I asked.

Rob smiled walking away with the empty cup.

"You can stay here if you want," an audible sound came from the kitchen.

"You can stay if you want," he repeated as he walked in with the second glass of water.

"Thanks," I answered.

"Thanks for the water or thanks for letting you stay?" he asked.

I looked up at him staring down at me. "Both," I replied with gratitude.

He smiled again. This time it was graceful, mercy was shown to me in that moment.

"Stay here," he commanded. "I'm going to prepare the guest room for you."

The house was massive. Rob walked off and after a while the footsteps were gone, lost in the distance of the many doors, I got up from the seat and stood in the middle of the room, filled with wonder about which direction to go in. I was ready to disobey direct orders left for me. Curiosity warmed my body till I couldn't take it anymore. So I opened the box, the ones located in the back of my mind and allowed Pandora to escape. I took a few steps towards a glass vase located beside a table by the fire place. The fire blazed beautifully, the flames danced like a traditional ceremonial ritual. As I approached it, the demon in my head dared me to touch it. The voice was quite persistent and I was foolish enough to listen, and I didn't have the energy to say no. My large slippery fingers moved to touch the vase, and squeezed between a second vase. It was smaller but looked just as expensive as the first. My fingers stroked it, only too hard, knocking it over on to the floor with a smashing sound that penetrated my ear drums. I jumped in fright, worried and afraid of what Rob would say. I proceeded to pick up the pieces. Many as they were, I tried. I wasn't sure where the broom was so I used my hands to scoop up the little pieces and ended up cutting myself in the process.

"Is everything okay in there?" was the cry coming from the other room. He must have heard what happened.

"Ermmm," was the only word I could find as the question surprised me. I stuttered as the English language failed me; there were no words to be found. I couldn't find it to come out. Only gibberish left my tongue to find the blankness of Rob stepping into the room. Even at the mercy of my friend I still couldn't find the words to explain how and why I had not just sat there, waited and kept my hands to myself. The voice in my head laughed again, causing a semi-grin to be plastered on my face. It was like I was being controlled from inside out.

"The room is ready!" Rob announced. The tone in his voice suggested that he didn't know how best to respond and deal with the situation, so he didn't. He only continued to say, "There is also a change of clothes on the bed if you want."

My body took a sudden change in temperature, I felt loved again, wanted and cared for, something that has neglected me for the longest of while, the thought ended with a *"thank you"* as I gave him an awkward smile.

"Thank you for being a great friend," I ended, before picking up again.

"I stayed away from you because...." Rob interrupted me as I was to explain.

"You don't have to explain," he said, allowing me to close my mouth.

"Thank you," I uttered again while walking down the hall way towards the room prepared for me. I stepped in the room, dropped the clothes off my back and went straight into the shower. My body felt that rest was near. I lifted the clean clothes from off the bed and placed them on the floor and slummed straight on the bed and fell asleep.

That night was the best sleep I had in a long while. Although it was great, it was rudely interrupted by a familiar face, a familiar dream, the dead fox that I had hit previously had come back to greet me. I couldn't say he was dead because his eyes were still moving. He kept following me, but I was sure he was dead. I thought that maybe he was a zombie. In the dream, the fox was chasing me and he was able to speak in English and it was plain and clear. He was not asking for redemption. All he wanted justice for his death. The fox had no skin around his jaws, therefore exposing his sharp small teeth. It looked like it was ready to cut through flesh. I ran frantically and hid behind a building. It was dark and the wind was strong. I was able to smell him as he got closer. I was well out of sight as the fox dizzily looked for me. I could see him but he couldn't see me. He only had one eye ball in tack and I wasn't sure if the other one hanging from his face was still working. He was chanting, "You shall not escape me this time! You shall not escape me! There is nowhere you can run that I will not find you!" The building I was hiding in was an old school building. It looked like it was burnt down some time ago. Grey bricks decorated its outer layer. Overgrown grass crept on the walls. The place looked like no one had been there in years. The thought ran in my mind then I quickly brushed it away. Was there any resemblance with the fox and the voice? I wondered. They seemed to be saying the same things to me. Sweat ran down the bridge of my nose. I stuck my tongue out as it dropped on to my bottom lip. It tasted like a bitter fruit or fear. The nerves bit me like a deep chill, but I never once showed my face. Afraid, yes, definitely afraid, but it was all about surviving as the dead fox relentlessly marched around in a circle looking for me. The fox made an announcement that sounded like a threat! He said, "You are going to die soon, and I will be there to watch it, in the eddy of the crowd, look for my face, before vanishing into thin air!" I looked around the corner and he was gone. Scared the monster was hiding, I also stayed hidden for a little longer just in case. When the time finally came I stood up and walked out of the school gates, hearing them clatter and shut behind me was a sound I will not forget. It sounded like prison gates shutting. I woke up in a pool of liquid, checking to see if I had wet the bed, I ran my hand across the pants I had put on during the night as it got colder, it was sweat I reviled. I got up instantly to the sight on the clock that read 4am. I slipped my shoes on and left Rob's house, he was still asleep, the dream was all the warning I needed to take Rob away from the danger that followed me. I was careful not to make a sound, I stepped out of a dark place and straight into another as the sun was still hiding. I walked down the road in the direction I had come the previous day. My hood was flung over my head as it hung to the floor. I reached the end of the road. As I looked back up at Rob's house, a feeling of fragmented promises haunted me, there's one last thing I must do.

"I am very sorry," I pled, faintly, in hope that the wind would carry my words to the sleeping ears of my good friend.

CHAPTER 17

A bright ray of sunlight caught my eye as I walked along the highway, and I stopped for a moment to only admire the beauty that life had to offer. I wondered if the sun would set on me again, as it does the day a child enters the world, and I dreamed of feeling its warmth one last time. I wanted to bask in it. The morning was just as chilly as the day before. The only difference was that the sun was out; familiar British weather, I thought, trapped in a labyrinth of thoughts that would carry my feet to a bridge. I stood on the edge peering at the metallic sea of cars beneath me.

"Help!" I whispered a wordless cry. I repeated the call, except this time a louder cry came out, alerting the birds to rise to the sky in fear.

"If you are real I need your help!" I continued. "Is anyone there?" I shouted.

I was to receive an answer filled with silence of nothing. The hooded jumper that covered my body also covered my face from any onlookers that dared to peak at death. As I walked along the bridge, I feared falling but I wanted to fall. I had no courage to throw myself off but I was waiting on an accident to happen something that would authenticate that my time is now. I felt my soul as it left my body, riding on the back of the wild wind whistling. I felt lower than a man, a subhuman if you may say; I wanted the pain to go away; I needed it to go away. I loved Nicole but if I was able to trade places with her I would, I would let her feel the pain and allow the maggots to eat me from inside out. Fair trade, I wondered as I stood at the edge of the bridge stretching as far as me hand could take me as if my head was in the clouds flying. The air smelt fresh, light and tasteless. For a moment I thought I was gone, that my foot had slipped, knocking my knee against the metal bar that separated the two pillars, but I regained balance and held on.

A musical orchestra played below me as the sound of horns blew. I suspected that they were trying to alert the authorities of my presence on the edge of the metal beam separating my quantum being from the flurry of fast-moving cars. Some said to jump while others were a bit more compassionate as they waved their hands in a criss-cross motion to signal, 'don't.' I wasn't doing it for them. I was doing it for me. I needed to. I made eye contact with one of the drivers passing by. Time seemed to have slowed down, stood still perhaps. I carefully took my next step and gazed into his eyes; I found no joy. My thoughts also slowed while the voice sat back.

I could feel him in the back of my cranium; he felt like a lump visible to the outside world. Although he wasn't to say a word, I knew he was there waiting on the right time to strike. He watched closely. I could feel his eyes burning a hole in the front of my head. I wondered why he didn't say a word, laugh or even smile. The bridge rocked and swayed as the strength of the silent wind tested the structure. I closed my eyes and was able to find him in the complex maze of my brain. He was in the Centre of a room. The room was upside down, and chairs were on the side of the wall while the tables were on the roof. The whole room was in a different order; it was strange. I peeked through the crack of my eyelid a few times to make sure I could still control that.

The room was half-filled with water while the other half was on fire. I fully opened my eyes as the wind speed picked up on the bridge.

I hung on tighter than before but was still there. I didn't want to leave the world, but the world was rejecting me.

"What am I supposed to do?" I asked myself.

I closed my eyes again, and there he was, seated in one of the chairs on the wall. He looked straight at me, deep into my eyes. I broke eye contact with him, afraid it would permanently keep me fixed to the upside-down house. I was standing at the doorway. If I took a step forward, I would fall into the water,, and if I stayed there any longer, the fire would consume me. I feared fire.,

I took my attention away from the fear of being burned, and when I refocused it, he was in my face. I felt frightened and jumped like when a person has a falling dream and suddenly wakes up with both feet planted on the floor.

"This is what you have wanted all along?" I asked, not loudly or aggressively but just enough so he could hear me.

Frankly, I was tired of fighting, so I said it in a soft tone that represented a lamb: innocent and subtle. His eyes narrowed in on me as a sniper does his next target. He opened his mouth, but no word came out. I anticipated an onslaught, but none came. Ever since I told the old man my problem, the voice sounded different. It was like he was choosing his words carefully, or dare I say it, but afraid. I reopened my eyes and took a few more steps back and forward. I turned to jump and then held on again.

"You need to be in an institution!" someone shouted above all the noise.

It was the morning rush hour, meaning the vast number of people going to be out was a lot as another stampede would begin—a typical day for a place like this. The bridge was located just minutes from where I used to live and about an hour from where I came from. I wanted to jump, but I needed to clear my mind.

"Jump!" someone in the passing crowd shouted.

I kept silent with my head facing down; I didn't want anyone to see the shame on my face. The commotion gathered pace, and more and more people gathered around me. I felt like I was boxed in a cage, and I was the lab rat. They were all watching to see if the experiment had worked or if I was to change my mind about jumping. I certainly couldn't at that point.

The police were called as well as the ambulance. I heard a lady on the phone say, "There's a crazy man on the Charlotte bridge and he looks like he is about to jump!"

I looked at her in hope that my stare would strike her where she stood. She realised her fate, turned around, walked away, and continued with the phone at her ears. I took a seat on the edge of the bridge, dangling my feet over, peeping to the bottom as if I was checking the distance, it would take a minute or so before I splattered on the ground. I figured I wouldn't die straight away, and it would be painful. It would be slow, and I would ask for it to go away. There was a reason I chose rush hour; I wanted to be hit by one of the cars.

"Instant kill," I said to my weak self.

The voice was back to his seat on the side of the wall. This time he had a drink in his hand, slurping, stirring the ice with a straw, being a nuisance, yet still no words from him. He closed his mouth for a moment as he took in the attention.

The sirens played a sweet melodious tune. It reminded me of the fire. I was small, but I could remember the sound well. I remember I was in college, and Rob was there. Back in those days, we were inseparable. I had an afro while he enjoyed his clean cut. I was always afraid of heights, and to a degree, I still am. I remember we took flight to the school's top floor, managed to find a way past the locked roof door, and sat there. I remember the wind beating against my face, making me look left and right simultaneously. I hung on for my life; it was Rob's idea to go up there.

Another kid had followed us up there. We had no association with him; he simply saw an opening, leaped, and followed us to the top. He walked along the edge, almost unaware of the danger. Despite our pleas for him to get down, he didn't stop. He continued to walk until his leg found a crack in the roof, kicked it, and tripped. He slid halfway down the roof, kicking and screaming for help. Time slowed down for me as I watched him slide to his death; he had no chance of survival. He fell to the ground and was twisted up in a spaghetti-shaped mess. We removed ourselves from the roof. The school found out that we were up there as well and were suspended for two weeks.

„Hey," someone said in a soft and gentle voice. "Don't do this," he said convincingly, increasing his voice to overpower the chatting from the crowd.

The young man continued to move through the crowd and said, "life has so much meaning to it. If only you saw the beauty in all the troubles, the darkness, the trips, and the bruises. Wounds can be so painful, it's a mess. I know life is tough, I know, but you're tougher than it is. Look on the bright side my friend."

He called me a friend like I was his friend. I knew he was lying and only saying empty words that were only heavy enough to fill a fool's mind.

"Look on the bright side," he repeated.

I stood back up from the seated position I had so comfortably taken up. I began to take a few steps closer towards the helping voice.

"What lovely words," I said in a sarcastic tone. I wasn't trying to be disrespectful. I wasn't, but I was finding it hard to trust the words of others.

"Nicole once told me she would always be here, now where is she?" I looked around as if that search was still ongoing.

"You will be missed if you go ahead and do this," the young man interjected.

I broke eye contact with the man and looked into my mind. I only found the figure of the voice seated on the edge of his chair. Tension and anxiety had built up, and the show was just starting to get interesting. The voice murmured as he broke the silence that held his tongue like a vice. The police took their turn to try and convince me that the sensible thing to do was to get down, but I ignored and refused their request. A few ladies and elderly people stepped up to the task, and all their efforts were shut down by the 'crazy man' as I had accepted the label. All I wanted was to be loved, never to be lonely, to feel wanted. Now, look at what has been created because of the menace in my head.

"Jump," he said in a loud voice.

The vibration of the word made the bridge shake. The cables holding the weight twitched as if they had been weakened by the command, 'jump'.

"If only you knew my story," I began my plea, bringing the decibels of my voice above all the chatter of the uncaring but present flock. "What would you have done differently?" I asked.

I gave them no context for my story. I wanted them to know me, but I was afraid of what life would have done. It is cruel, dangerous, and savage. You have to be able to take yourself away from the turmoil and the pace of life. Just to reconnect, clear your mind, recharge your batteries and be prepared to go again.

"I knew what I was supposed to do," I sighed, "but I just wasn't able, I didn't have the strength. I was mentally weak, I now hate the world but want people. I realised that a world without connection with people is a world lived alone. No matter how many happy moments you have created, connection with people is needed. On all levels, work, personal, family and sexually. That's what I was truly missing."

My head dropped, showing my disappointment and for a moment, I forgot I was on a bridge. I let go of the grip I had tightly held and held out my hand as an angel would. I felt the wind on my back. It cushioned me as I started to fall back. I remembered there was silence around me. I whispered the words sorry a few times to no one in particular. Maybe I felt sorry for the fact that I was to waste a precious life that was so beautifully made. The police had already stopped traffic below, so I had to improvise. My head was positioned to hit first, and I felt my body getting lighter as I broke through the wind like a knife through butter.

"Stop!" a voice shouted as I felt a hand on my chest. It grabbed a load of my shirt and balanced me as my feet were still planted on the beam. My heart was beating like it was trying to escape from my chest. I breathed like I had just run a mile. I was halted by the hands of the old man.

The voice in my head was now filled with rage; it was like he had lost a championship game in the dying seconds. I closed my eyes to picture him, and everything was being knocked off the table as he rose to his feet. It was an angry rise, like a spring compressed for an extended period of time, waiting to be free. He wasn't happy I hadn't jumped. He snarled out an exaggerated 'NOOO!!'. Disbelief covered him; a fragile old man had come to save me. The sight of the old man had caused the voice to go into rampage mode.

I didn't see it as being saved. I still wanted to jump. I was angry at him for turning up. For once, I was in agreement with the voice. We wanted me to jump. I took a few steps away from the edge of the beam, standing at first, then reluctantly sitting on the bridges concrete structure. I wasn't entirely away, but I was far enough so that people could retake their breaths for a moment at least. The old man stepped closer to me, and I could feel his energy as it got closer. I felt it hug me; it was warm. The adrenalin left my body and was replaced by the goosebumps caused by the ever-bitter wind that blew. In the back of my ear, I heard the old man say, "take my hand."

I gave him no response, and then the same line came out, prompting me to react and answer perhaps. All I did was turn to him and look into his caring eyes. He called out my name, causing my hand to react. It stretched out as if I was to grab him; then, I didn't. I stood back up, shifting closer to where I was. The old man's face dropped. I could see the disappointment in the lines of his brows.

The old man stepped forward as if he wanted to join me.

"I know how you're feeling Andreas, I really do," he cried out.

I could hear the fear in the tone of his voice.

"How could someone I barely know care about me so much?" I asked myself.

"It was all strange to me," he continued. "I have been through the same thing you are going through. There were no more tears to pour out of my eyes. That wasn't me any more, in a sense the voice was right, I needed to find the strength. There is always another way," the old man pleaded. "I am living proof of that!" he shouted.

The attempt of shouting was a roar that trickles like a new born lion cub, tame. But I heard it nonetheless.

"Please take my hand," he continued.

There was compassion found in the words that came out. I sat back down, still on the edge, but this time lowering the weapon I possessed, free will. The old man sat next to me. The wind gently blew over us as I gazed in the distance, hoping it would be strong enough to carry the wish I was making. The crowd was still standing, watching as if they were watching a movie. The slow-moving traffic passed by, peering out of the window. Perhaps they were looking out of the fantasy they had previously created and into the real world. What if the image they saw was an expression of the state of the weak crying out for help? What if we were to remove the caste system created by the elites and flipped it upside down? Was he any stronger than me for not facing his fears?

"I think not," I thought to myself.

Others had their phones out recording, waiting for the punchline, the grand finale, the closing act. The action is what they wanted. That is why they paused their busy lives for me. A member of the crowd had previously said, "Jump."

"enough of the dialogue," others whispered. A few dispersed as it dragged on for nearly an hour.

"Do you feel sad?" was the question asked.

I looked at him and gave a gentle nod. No eye contact was made; there was always a stigma about admitting to problems. I bought into that idea as well, society had filled my head with their hashtag goals, and I followed. I wasn't used to the attention, and circumstances had changed me. The moment seemed silent like we were in an empty room. It felt like a barn in the middle of the countryside, and all that was present was the sound of the winds hitting the trees. The old man continued,

"I hate when sadness takes over me," it seemed like a speech was on its way, like when Nicole used to say, "can I have a word with you?".

"The energy that drives me disappears," the old man persisted, directing his voice in the direction of my face as it dropped. "The frequency that flows gets muddled up, I need that," he took a moment as if he was thinking of the words to say. "umpth," as he connected and found it, "the imagination, the battery cell that catapults me into action, and into this fantasy we called a world. The worst times are when I feel lonely and there is no connection."

I started to take note as my ears perked up like an antenna. The old man shuffled his bum; maybe it was getting numb. The lecture picked back up:

"Those are the worst times," he said. "Not even a phone call or a positive word from a book or a billboard could change that mood. The signal had been cut, cut away from the source, flat lined," he continued, referring to death itself. "It's a horrible place to be. It's tough, but you have to endure it. You have to embrace the feeling and allow it to pass," he turned towards me with a somewhat fixated focus.

He told me to allow it to enter and then swiftly exit. To give the thought no time to settle, reminding that the thought that it doesn't define me.

"You don't determine who I am. You must take a back seat to this feeling. On this roller-coaster ride. You are just a passenger, not the driver. You are not the feeling itself, separate the two. Gravitate to the things that bring you joy, remember them!" the old man demanded and tapped his fingers on the front of my head. "Remember them!" he repeated. "Apply faith, because you don't know how things are going to work out. You just know that they will."

I sat by the edge of the bridge looking at the old man. Everything that was just said was received. I heard it loud and clear. It was a message I needed to hear. The old man spoke to my soul. My eyes widened as I searched for grace. It was like I was high on some kind of drugs; except I was high on the words of wisdom shared. This was the grace I had begged for. I gazed around as if I was wandering in the forest of the galaxy.

"Take my hand," the old man rejoiced, this time sensing a weakness in my desire to jump.

I stretched out my hand to him, and within seconds, I was off the bridge. The crowd cheered as my feet touched down. Some just simply walked away as if they had just lost a bet. The police tightened the handcuffs around my arms and took me in for questioning. Nothing was found wrong; evaluations were normal. The voice didn't want to be stuck in a mental hospital, so he kept his mouth shut. The old man took me in as his guest. Staying with the old man was the closest to home I was to get, so I took it with both hands.

CHAPTER 18

A deadly silence woke me from my sleep, it was a welcomed change from the usual voice playing thunderous tunes in my head. I laid in the bed for a little while longer, having neither the energy nor the passion for getting up. I rolled from my back to the side that faced the window. The frost built up on the window, causing me to think back to the night on the streets. I closed my eyes and rolled back to the other side. I didn't want to think of it any longer.

Nicole was still on my mind as she always was. I couldn't get her out even if I had tried. It had only been a couple of months which felt like days. She betrayed me, but I still loved her. I planted my face into the pillow. I wanted it to swallow me. I counted to ten, then rose to the side of the bed, this time sitting on the frame. The bed was small; if I had rolled a second time, I would have fallen off. The springs in the bed made a sound each time I moved, and my weight sunk into the middle. Despite all that, I was ever grateful for the compassion shown to me.

I rose to my feet somewhat lazily. I felt like I was just learning how to walk again. My days of teaching Shakespeare sprung to mind. I walked around the room as the story of Macbeth appeared. The desire Macbeth showed to get what he wanted inspired me, he stopped at no cost. I was to decide whether to stay in this house or leave the sovereignty of the nest created for me by the voice. As I was picking up the pieces of my life, I remembered a poem that I had written for Nicole. I remembered it so well I began to recite it in a small, tender tone. I peered out the window of the room, watching shadows follow their leaders, step, by step, hoping the words I uttered would somehow bring Nicole back,

Like a sculpture shining with perfection
beautiful, and yet so charming, loving, and still so intelligent,
life's full of imperfections, but your heart reminds me
of no complications,
you are a wonderful design,
created by the hands of the maker
fit for a place among the heavenly
your beauty outshines the stars,
and curves like the goddess of the sky,
sensitive but calm, unique and luscious,
precious and so talented,
upright and rigid, elegance is your way,
like a sculpture, she sits and stares,
like a sculpture, she has no care,
Nicole is her name.

The words rang in my ears as I they left my lips. Her face was the only image I could see. The way she walked, talked, it was all coming back to me like it was only yesterday I was with her. I stroked the window with my opened fingers, leaving a trail of four lines. I imagined it was the bulge of her cheek. I remembered the way she used to look at me. I remembered the soft parts in her eyes as they sparkled during the best times, the gentle slant of her head as the words fell out of her lips. It was like she had just been kissed. She licked her lips at times as if she was tasting me, then looked into my eyes as she held my chest.

I recalled it so clearly; my unconscious minds mystic, almost cryptic messages pressed replay and lit a fire within. I loved her, I hate her, I repeated this sequence hoping to stop on hate, but I couldn't. I needed another to take her place, I wanted to forget her.

I walked away from the window to the door leading out to the living area. I opened the door and was in pursuit of the old man. It didn't take me long as I found him on the floor meditating. He looked peaceful, and not even my heavy footsteps could break the stillness of the master. I owed him my life. I was due to make a big mistake. One that I would not be able to have a second chance at doing over again.

The aura surrounding the old man was inviting, so I invited myself beside him. The seat was a thin cushion on the floor. After sitting for only a minute, my bum was numb, it was painful, but I was still seated. My posture was not mirroring that of the man opposite me. I was unsure of what to do, so I tried to copy what I saw. The old man had his fingers interlaced and his eyes closed. I remembered a little from the meditation book I once read, and I was doing it wrong. The breathing technique, the channelling of energy, and the thought process. The old man opened his mouth, giving me a fright, and said,

"Allow the thoughts to enter your mind and flow straight through only giving them the awareness and then move on."

I forcefully opened my eyes to see the words floating around the living area. I had a confused look on my face as the words connected not. It made sense, I thought. The old man repeated it with a slight difference, the tone was different. It was like he was saying it to match the flow of water running down a river. It was slow, rhythmic and it had a beat to it. This time I understood, I re-sealed my eyes and allowed thought to flow. I was getting it. He cheered with only a smile on his face. I half-opened one eye to see if the old man was watching; he wasn't. He was focused on his mission. I closed my eyes once more and began to think.

The voice appeared in my head, and he seemed beaten up. He felt weak and spoke with uncertainties. The fact that I did not jump from that bridge must have strengthened me and lessened him. I felt my energy level going up. I gave another smile, this time, I didn't open my eyes. I kept to the task. The voice continued to speak; this time, he was walking towards me. I stood there, and as he got close enough, I squeezed my eyes tighter, slamming a door shut and separating him from me. I could still hear him but not see him. His voice was faint, almost unheard. I allowed the thought to escape from my mind, and the door was shut. The key was in my pocket, and I was in control of it.

I opened my eyes to the smell of the fresh bakery coming from across the road. It took me to a sensational place, a place where everything was right—with the lines of my mouth like sand from a desert. I needed something to eat or at least wet the base of my tongue. I didn't have the strength to allow the thought to pass. Instead, it carried me away like I was in food heaven. My imagination ran wild as I sat there. My eyes were open, staring in the distance. I wasn't focusing on anything, in particular, just gazing. I felt my mouth open and drool as I wished what I wanted.

"Full English," I said to myself as I gave a smile.

I felt light and free; there was to be no interruption running through my head. The wind blew a flat, crisp breeze in my face that tore me away from my wonders. I was feeling the energy, and it electrified my body. The control was real; I felt it through the air I breathed in. The blood that pumped through my veins was renewed. I wasn't over Nicole, but I was not about to kill myself; that chapter was now over.

A sound tweeted through the window. It was a familiar sound. One I could resonate with—the sound of the birds that usually congregate at my window. I felt like they found me. Even though I had not gone very far, it seemed as though they wanted me to fly with them. I thought about the idea many times,

“Maybe one day when I have closed the book of my life I will fly with you,” I said as I gazed at them.

No sound was to leave my mouth; the old man was still focused. I even wondered if he was sleeping. The birds stayed by the window for another twenty minutes before flying off. I rose to my feet and walked to the kitchen. The old man opened his eyes and, without turning his head, asked in a tone that suggested he knew the answer already,

“You're hungry?” the question hidden behind a statement caught me by surprise, so I stuttered out a response: “How did you know?”

He shaped his face as if he was about to smile, then stopped and said, “I could hear your stomach as I was meditating.”

The old man got up and walked to the kitchen. He didn't say a word as he walked past me. I was starting to understand him; he didn't say much. He only spoke when necessary, and when he did speak, it was always straight to the point profound and meaningful. My numb feet followed behind him like a puppy wagging his tail in wait for food. My stomach rumbled like that of Bombay drums. They were playing a song entitled, ‘I want food.’ The old man turned and looked over his left shoulder as he chopped tomatoes and onions,

“How are you doing this morning?”

I sighed as I broke eye contact with him before giving a reply that could seem good or bad. “I'm doing fine,” I said.

“I hope so,” he added, “you was in a pretty bad state yesterday.”

I nodded as if I was too embarrassed to say anything else. He continued to cook something for me. I didn't know what it was, but the smell rubbed my stomach as if to caress it.

“I feel good,” I said, finding the courage to talk about how I felt.

I'm in a better place. I feel like the demon is off my back. The frustration took shape along the creases of my face. I brushed it aside as a means to nothing. Flabbergasted and amazed with myself, this was a moment to savour. It was one to remember years to come. Maybe this was the sort of achievement I needed to encourage me. I was sure the voice was about to cause yet another catalyst of turmoil. I looked at my hands and thought to pinch myself. *Was I still asleep?* I questioned.

Without making a sound, my face told the story. I need not say a word as the joy was seeping through my paws. The old man was not watching, but then he turned, almost with suspicion of knowing. He looked straight through me. I gulped, but the ball in my throat was too large, so it got stuck at the top of my throat. It caused me to cough violently,

"This was a weird feeling," I thought. "Can he even see me?" I marvelled as I tried to regain control of my breathing.

I continued to interrogate my own sanity. All the while, my stomach was still grumbling.

"Has the voice taken physical form?" I asked as I shook my head vigorously to answer the question, unaware that it would make any difference. As if that would make the truth untrue. "The voice was defeated," I murmured loud enough so that the old man could get a peep of the sound travelling through the empty flat.

We looked at each other, and a smile cracked on our faces. I opened my mouth and announced, "This is the end of it," I proclaimed it into existence and continued, "He brought me to the brink of defeat. He wanted me to die." My voice was desolate at that point: "His desire and determination weren't enough to end my life!" I exulted. "I can see clearly now as my eyes have widened. The purpose that was once very close to my heart has now returned. As long as I have breath flowing through my nostrils," I announced as loud and deep as my voice could carry, "I will fulfil my dreams! I have new meaning; the world needs someone like me! I have realised the errors I have been making all along. People are wonderful beings and connections are a way of life, like plants connect to the earth, we too need to connect to each other."

"The voice will never fully go," the old man jumped in, soiling my mood, "he will always be there lingering in the back ground and though he wont be as strong you will still hear him. The only difference is that you have the power now, he doesn't control you." The old man paused for a second; he was stirring the pot but stopped the motion half way through. The next time he spoke, his tone was gloomy, dense and felt like the sound of thunder outside. "You have to be careful not to neglect the voice in your head, as much as it is a problem also note that it is also very important that you continue to check on it. It is a weaker version of who you are now. In another dimension the roles could have been reversed and you would have been the demon," he continued. "Meditation is important, but ask yourself questions to see if your state of mind is ok, build your inner strength such that nothing external can affect you." He stopped almost abruptly without warning. His words penetrated the depths of my subconscious being and laid there comfortably. That day, I would later come to realise that the words of the old man were the truest things I have ever heard. The old man struck a smile as his fingers clung against a glass on the kitchen counter. I looked across the room questionably. My eyes circled the kitchen for signs of when the food would be ready. The kitchen was just like all the other rooms, simple, uncomplicated and had almost nothing. The old man lived a completely different life from what I was used to and through him I was given a second chance at life.

"I am forever in your debt," I uttered this time the words came out tickling the old man's ears and he responded with a simple gaze, a slight turn of the head, his eyes connected with mine, then a faint nod of the head.

A few hours later I was outside. The frost in the air was sharp and dangerous enough to bring the body in to shock. The warmth of my breath connected with the dryness of the outside air and made a cloud of smoke in front of me as I exhaled some fresh air. The air smelt different; lighter and garden fresh. My strides were short, as I glided across the pavement like an ice skater dominating the ring - it seemed as though time slowed down and it most definitely suited me because I felt weightless as we walked in no particular direction, just a matter of stretching our legs greeting every passer-by with a gentle welcoming smile. It was a weird feeling for me as this was something I would never have done in the past. I hated most of the people I saw and if Nicole was to see me now, she would turn in her grave or maybe formulate a smile of relief. Either way this was not me but I felt good inside and I liked it and so I continued.

Our feet carried us to a local grocery store. The store front was really pretty; well, that was the only word I could find in the back of my mind as I searched for something to describe perfection. The old man sat on a stool outside as I wandered in. I walked round the shop aimlessly looking for nothing in particular, after all I had no money. The shop was well organised, clean and fresh. I walked from aisle to aisle as a means of passing time and along the way I stumbled across a young lady who couldn't have been more than twenty five. I watched her as she elegantly moved along the aisle packing the shelves single handed and on her head she wore two afro buns. She had thick beautiful hair that one would wish they had but could never afford. Her skin was rich in melanin, smooth as silk and she had hazelnut brown eyes. She was bent down on her knees as she filled the bottom shelve and when she rose, I figured she couldn't have been more than five feet five in height.

I watched her as she moved and I stared at her in pure amazement. My jaws dropped and I drooled in confusion at what was happening to my stomach. All that was on my mind was that this lady was exquisitely beautiful. I watched her tentatively and penetrated her with my thoughts as I tried to wonder if her insides were as aesthetically appealing as her outward appearance. She moved down the aisle towards my direction, her eyes making contact with mine as I gave her an awkward smile. I felt her laughing, since she saw a weakness in me and this weakness was her. I clumsily said good morning as she got closer, it was faint and I wasn't sure she even heard me as no response came out of her mouth. She took another step closer and asked me if I was okay.

"Do you need any assistance?" she asked again.

"No; are you the owner of the store?" I fired back.

"Yes, my grandmother used to own it and after she died, she passed it down to me."

I gave her a smile to signify a hug to a loved one. We had only just met but I thought she deserved it. I stood beside her as she continued to pack swaying from side to side as if I were a school child talking to a girl for the first time. Her eyes connected with mine and I melted.

"Amazing," I said out loud.

She laughed then asked, "What's amazing?" I froze and said nothing. The bell above the door of the shop rang as a customer entered. He stood by the counter waiting for service and the beautiful lady left to the aid of the man. I stood there and watched her as she walked off. She strutted down the aisle like it was a run way, one foot in front of the other as if she was a model. I was in awe. I waited until the man had left the counter before approaching her, I asked her if she needed any help in the store and to my surprise she said yes with a faint smile that only rose from the corner of her mouth. I returned the smile.

"I will come back tomorrow morning to help," I blurted out. The excitement was too much to contain. I asked for her number before leaving which got stored in my phone under the name of, I paused as I remembered I didn't ask her name. I looked at her and was only able to smile. I sighed.

"I'm sorry but I didn't ask you your name."

She let out a small giggle and said, "Naomi."

"Beautiful name," I uttered.

"And yours?" she asked.

"Andreas," as I left the shop the sight of the old man deep in conversation with another old man caught my eye. I was worried I had left him alone for too long but he was fine. I let the old man know that I was going for a walk down a street I was very familiar with. I walked along the pavement kicking a stone from my path. The air from that point on tasted sweet and it reminded me of the big breakfast the old man made. The spring in my steps were bouncy and all I could think about was how to break the good news to the old man. I knew he would be so proud of me for getting back on my feet. I smiled as the words cross my mind. The walk became sweeter with each step I took and so I continued down the road.

A lady from across the road shouted my name and it was followed by coughs; deep violent coughs.

"Andreas!" the distant voice said as it got closer and closer. The voice sounded familiar but I couldn't quite place who it belonged to. I racked my brain trying to match the voice to a face but the person was too far away to recognise. All I managed to concluded was that it was a woman.

I narrowed my eyes as I tried to peer through the crowded set of people along the pavement. That didn't help, why was she shouting my name from so far I wondered as it started to annoy me. I wanted to hide from her but she was locked on to my location already. I could tell by the way she moved, confident, fast and deliberate. I looked away in embarrassment. The slender figure got closer as the vivid mirage became clearer.

"It's Lisa from the school," I said as the light bulb above my head lit up. She seemed different, I thought. The look on my face may have seemed rude but her appearance caught me by surprise. It seemed like she had been drinking, drugs maybe or maybe she was ill I thought to myself as I tried to stop being judgemental. She didn't look right and certainly not how I last saw her. She had now gotten close enough to start a conversation and she took the first chance she got. Her lips moved and said something but I missed it as she spoke fast and off beat and my focus had shifted to her stench. It confirmed what I was suspicious about, the smell of alcohol was poking my face.

"How are you doing?" I asked hesitantly, trying to take my mind off the smell. She completely ignored the question and followed up with a question of her own, it was the same question I had just asked. I ignored the slightly rude act and answered her question. I didn't tell her much just that I was fine and doing well. She was well aware of the condition I had. She knew that the voice was a big problem in my life. Either way I continued to entertain and tell her that I had changed my life. I let her know that I had gone in a new direction. She seemed like she was listening intently for an answer for her own life and if she was in a position to take note, she would. I asked the question again curious to find out what happened to her in these short few months I had not seen her and all she could do was give me an embarrassed look. I looked in her eyes but saw nothing. Not only did she look lost but the look in her face also said *don't ask me again, please.* It was a scary look and so I didn't force the issue. We walked along the busy street as we engaged in small talk. I asked her how the school was coming along, how everyone was coping including the students but again she ignored the question. I raised my eyebrows and was very confused. I wasn't sure what was going on or why was she ignoring my questions. I asked again but no answer was forthcoming which made things worse. As I was starting to assume horrible things, she turned to me and asked about my fiancé. This was a topic I wasn't ready to share especially with someone from my past and one that I wasn't close with. I ignored the question as I said hello to a familiar face.

"How are you doing?" I asked again as I demanded to know what the problem with her was. I had come to the conclusion and assumption that it was the alcohol causing her to behave like she did and chosen to give it a rest but this time she answered the question to my surprise. She said she was fine, I didn't believe her and even continued to say that she was just having a good time. I wasn't sure what she meant by "having a good time" but since I was tired of trying to get her to talk to me, I dropped the issue. We got to an intersection and parted ways. She walked off to the left and I went off to the right without uttering a word or even bidding each other goodbye. I shook my head, chuckled and looked at the clock in one of the shops. The old man must be missing me, I thought as I went back to where I had come from.

I walked up the creaking unstable stairs with the old man just in front and the old one-eyed dog by his side as usual. I was thinking of the weird encounter I had just had with my mind still on Lisa as I walked to the door of the house I once occupied. I was given the spare key by the old man and used it to let us in. I entered the flat and took a large breath of air and it sweetened my nostrils. We walked in and the old man went to his bedroom. He looked tired and pale. I asked him if he was OK and he answered in the affirmative as the door slammed shut behind him. I continued along the hall way into the living room and sat there for about an hour or so. All this while the dog was outside the old man's door as he usually was.

Excellent guard dog, I thought as I raised my head to confirm his position. After a few hours I knocked on the old man's door and asked him if he wanted some tea but I got no answer and so I asked again. Silence filled the gap between us and I suspected that something was wrong. I plastered my ears on the door to see if I could hear anything on the other side but I heard nothing. I was left with no choice but to burst through the door. The old man was on the floor, still breathing but in weird state. It seemed like he was in pain. He was curled up holding his chest as if he had just been shot. I quickly reached for my phone and called the ambulance and within fifteen minutes the ambulance was at the door. They burst into the room and pushed me away not so hard, in order for them to get access to the patient.

"Heart attack," I heard the tall, white one say.

"We need to get him to the hospital," the other said panic written all over their faces. My eye caught the many pictures on the old man's wall.

"His family." I thought as my eyes continued to circle the four walls. "Is that his wife?" I wondered as I took a step closer to see the beauty he so frequently described to me. She had dark brownish hair, small dark brown eyes with unusually large eyelashes.

She was beautiful. Even in her old age, I thought to myself. She stood in a field with her fingers trailing along the tall grass. The old man I assumed must have been the one who took the picture. The paramedics hoisted the old man onto the stretcher and carried him down the stairs. He wasn't a heavy man so they did it effortlessly though the stairs still creaked and I feared it would collapse causing greater damage to the unwell man. They placed him carefully into the ambulance and asked me if I was going to accompany them. I paused for a moment before taking a step inside. I was the only one he had and so I had no option other than to accompany him to a place I hated. I held his hand as the driver sped off. He didn't squeeze mine in return.

CHAPTER 19

The clock struck midnight and the sound of each passing second was noticeable. I sat by the old man's bed praying, chanting, wishing, and hoping for anything that would work. It wasn't like I believed in any God, but I really wanted someone to hear my cry. The knee joints were becoming weak from the nervous shake. The feeble figure of the old man lay on the hospital bed, his skin now paler than before. As his body lay motionless, I noticed a swelling around his shoulder area and assumed that that must have been where he hit as he fell. I felt the pain travel from his body to mine. He looked small and weak and I wondered how he had survived on his own for this long.

It had been five hours and thirteen minutes since we entered the hospital. I always hated hospitals because they always reminded me of death. In most cases no matter how well you entered, you would always exit worse if at all you did exit. I had a crazy phobia for hospitals and I always wondered which would be worst, the voice or being locked in here. The mere thought of it was chilling. I shook my head and, in the process, relieved all the garbage that I had collected. The smell was the other annoyance. It was the sort of smell that often hit the back of your nose until it leaked into the rearmost of your throat and I was forced to spit out the vile bile liquid. It always made me sick and I hated being here and if it wasn't for the love I had for the old man I would have left a long time ago.

I left his side to go to the toilet down the long sinuous hallway and when I had returned to my seat, my eyes caught the view of the outside world. We were on the twelfth floor and outside it was gloomy, dull and boring. I wondered if the old man's soul was going to leave with the birds I kept seeing. I turned around and looked at him lying on the bed once more. He looked like he was losing weight by the minute. I wondered if he was still in there. I moved to the side of the bed and was now talking to him. I thanked him for the help he had been providing me and begged him to not leave me. I stopped talking for a minute and wondered if the voice was doing all this. I closed my eyes as slowly as I could. I felt my heart skip a beat.

"The voice is gone," I told myself. I could not believe it. I was all alone with this joy and then the unexpected happened. The old man's fingers started to move! I felt the electricity flow through my body as a mixture of relief and excitement flowed with it. I called out to a nurse who was coincidentally walking past our room and she came running and checked the machine that was located to the rear of his bed. She did a couple more checks and broke into a smile. She looked at me and reassured me that everything was OK.

"Thanks," I said and stood to walk her out of the room. I noticed the medical records beside the bed; *Oranyan Adebisi* it said at the top of the paper work as I struggled to pronounce the difficult name. March 1938, 77 years old I noticed.

"You move well for a 77-year-old," I said, hoping he would hear me and tell me off for assuming he wasn't strong enough. The wrinkles on his face told his story, fears and struggles. I sat back down in the uncomfortable chair of the hospital, closed my eyes and within minutes was asleep.

The comfort of the chair was nothing to brag about, it was painful and harsh as it reminded me of when I slept on the street, except this time I was warmer. The doctors entered the room just as I was buttoning up the creased shirt I was wearing.

"We just have to run a few more test on him before we can consider discharging him," they announced.

"That is OK," I replied.

"Maybe by tomorrow he shall be out," they ended and walked back out. Oranyan was awake at this point and heard what had been said. His eyes lazily opened as if they were glued shut. He was calm as he usually was and looked at me in a somewhat worried way.

"Are you OK?" he inquired.

"I'm fine," I said as I stuttered the words out with a bewildered look on my face.

"I should be the one asking you that question," I added.

"Do you remember what happened?" I asked him. He shook his head left then right.

"I thought you were sleeping for too long which is not usually like you, so I went to your door to check you was OK but I couldn't hear a sound coming from your room. I knocked and - nothing, so I pushed the door open and your leg was obstructing the door so I had to push harder. So your the reason my leg is in such pain, he joked, I returned a half smile as the severity of the situation didn't warrant a full one. When I got in you were on the floor holding your chest and that is when I called the ambulance. I thought I heard them say heart attack, but I wasn't sure."

The old man's face slumped as he turned his head on the pillow to the side, looking sad and worried. It didn't strike me as a man that feared death, but I guess every man fears the time they have to say goodbye. I held his hand and told him, "it will be ok." He half smiled at my words.

"I have to go and finish something," I said. He turned his head back in my direction and gave me a look. His eyes slightly narrowed as if he was trying to figure out what I was up to. I realised he was trying to crack a puzzle and told him I was going to close a chapter in the book that I had left open. I was going to my parents' house to say goodbye properly. The old man sighed.

"You do what you have to son; just make sure you are safe."

I nodded for what seemed like an age, then stood up from the chair, walked to the door and stopped.

"I will be back before you know it," I said then walked through the door.

I stood outside the hospital gazing at nothing in particular, just wondering if I should leave the old man on his own or not.

What if something happens and no one is there to comfort him, I thought. What if....... I snapped out of the thought.

"I must do this. If everything is to completely end, I must do this," I repeatedly said to myself as if to reassure myself that what I was doing was the right thing. I walked away from the entrance of the hospital and down to the main road. The atmosphere was chilly, wet and bleak. I had my hood over my head and walked with my head down and occasionally I would look up. I reached the main road where the cab station was located.

"Where would you like to go?" the driver said.

"Olderman road," I replied, "where the road crosses the park." The driver turned around with a confused and perplexed look on his face suggesting not having a clue where I was talking about. I equally looked lost as I couldn't remember the postcode or any other details. I always knew how to get there, just never the actual address.

" Just head to Mayfield Ave in Southgate and I will direct you from there." The driver looked semi happy with those instructions and drove off. The cab got closer and I took over the navigation,

"At end of the road turn right," the driver followed.

"There is a roundabout coming up; go straight over," the driver followed.

"At the end of the road turn right and then pull over on your left," the journey was concluded.

"Thanks," I said as I dug my hand in my pocket to find the fare for the driver and handed it to him, I stepped out the cab and was right where it all started. I looked up at the house and it was beautiful. I remembered seeing pictures on the internet about a house burning down. Everything was to ashes and now look at it. Someone had made a home of it, moved in and done it up, nicely it must be said.

This is where it all ends, I thought.

"Closure must be had and doors must be closed," I continued.

As I got closer to the front gate I could hear screams and shouts. My heart skipped a beat and for a short moment I thought I could hear the screams of my parents burning. I put my hands to my ears and thought not again as screams stopped. It was the kids playing in the park. The shouts fizzled down to chatters of social media, play ground antics, who likes who and so on. My breathing went back to normal as the pressure that was building up was released before it could burst.

I approached the front gate as my body began to sweat as if it was having second thoughts. My palms were sticky like I had just dipped them in a tub of grease and felt as though a spirit had entered my body. The sensation was weird - though I had no words to explain the feeling, but I felt something. My legs was somewhat numb and weakened, leaving me stunned. I looked up at the reddened bricked house, and it was beautiful at first sight. I stood there watching, wishing things could have been different, but every man's path is chosen for a reason.

I looked at the sky and forgave Nicole and all those who had done me wrong – now my heart was clean; I had emptied it. I now realise Nicole was both my fear and my dream. I had to let one go. I was taken aback as I stood on the pavement watching the house like I was about to buy it. The area seemed like a nice place to live as it was clean and well-trimmed. I never dared entering the garden for fear of the consequences.

I looked like a thief stalking the place before the heist. The front garden was filled with flowers and was like a sea of green which reminded me of when my father used to bring mother velvet roses. The smile on her face told us to be careful around it. I remembered while taking a deep suck of air trying to locate the scent. I got closer to the gate as the memory made me feel comfortable. I trailed my fingers across the petals of the garden and was still hesitant to walk through the gate, but I needed to. The memories that plagued me for so long was no more a nightmare. I looked around as if I was seeking for help. I needed an excuse to get me through the gate and into the house. I needed to walk the halls of the house to feel the sensation left by the spirits of the ones I loved. I needed to feel the warmth of the bedrooms as well as step in the footsteps I once walked, but I was outside and it wasn't my house to go in. About half an hour went by and I didn't move no more than five feet away from the house. I thought many times whether I should break in with a simple nudge of the door. As big as the door was, it was easy to open.

A nice neighbourhood like this didn't need a lot of security, I thought, but many times I thought against it. My mind carried me over to the lady I had met at the grocery store, Naomi. She would of been a great help in a time like this. Her beauty would have been inviting, her sweet voice would have broken the barrier of my intimidating look.

The second time I said her name it was faint. I pushed the gate open, walked through the garden of roses discovering the hidden ones on the way past. I walked without a strategy and felt like I was contouring one step at a time.

"What was I to do if someone came out, or came in and saw a stranger in their front garden?" That question I wasn't able to answer.

The police would have been called, I thought as the inevitable loomed on me but continued anyway. My stature was bold and unafraid. I had taken the hardest step so far coming here in the first place. I stood at the front door, took a deep breath and smelt the air.

"Naomi," I whispered again as I remembered what I had promised her. I took my phone out of the depths of my pocket and texted her.

"I am very sorry I wasn't able to come to the store this morning. I had to attend to an emergency. If you are free next week, I would like to take you out to make it up to you."

I then clicked send. I felt good for letting her know. I was startled by the interruption of a woman who looked in her fifties. I rose to my feet in which I was seated and didn't know what to say. There wasn't anything I could say to justify being in someone else's front door. She entered the gate and was calmer than I thought she would be and it was only until later I realised she didn't notice me at first. I think it was because of the wall tree that travelled up and along the wall. She looked up and finally noticed me then jumped in a fright.

"I hope she doesn't have a heart attack," I thought.

"Hi!" I said breaking the dangerous silence while taking the bass out of my voice in the process.

She reluctantly replied with a trembled "hi!"

I began to explain why I was at her front door as she placed her shopping bags on the floor. It seemed as though she understood my feelings. The conversation carried on to the other side of the front door. I was in as I noticed the smell of the flowers were gone.

She allowed me in.

I thought as I was taking my shoes off trying to be as polite as possible. I felt a coldness down my spine but this time the feeling was not to evade me. I knew this feeling. The feeling you get when you are on a first date with the woman of your dreams; your stomach starts to twist and knot. Nerves intercepted the words from my tongue. I felt like I had walked through a thin wall of water vertically held up by the force pulling them on opposite ends.

"Would I be able to walk through the house," I asked as polite as I possibly could.

The lady said, "yes!" to my surprise.

I started with the upstairs rooms. I walked along the stairs dragging my fingers along the wall and the lady stepped with me. I looked over my shoulder and noticed the cautious figure of this woman following me. It was chilling, but I was grateful for her allowing me to close the doors left opened. I reached the top of the stairs and pictures plastered all over the walls reminded me of the family I desired so much. I entered the first bedroom to the left which was a large room.

"The master bedroom," I wondered, "was it my parents' room?" I asked myself.

I leant against the frame of the door way. My eyes dreamed as they circled the room looking for familiar memories. I took a step back out of the room then closed the door behind me. There was no connection as things felt distant and disconnected. I didn't know what I was hoping for. Frustration covered me like a blanket and the sound of little feet running at pace along the hall way played in my head. The sound travelled to the room directly opposite the one I just exited.

"Was that my room?" I wondered.

There was a spark of connection starting to happen and the dots were being drawn. The sound was of me running from my room to my parents' room.

The excited little feet, I thought as a smile was pained across my face. "I used to run to the comfort of their safety, my love and protectors," I sighed. They were no longer here as tears settled in the centre of my eyes as if I were to blink they would fall. I quickly wiped it away hoping it was not noticed and slowly turned my head in embarrassment, but she had noticed. The lady had caught the emotions flowing from my eyes to my cheeks. She stepped away to get a tissue.

"Thanks," I said as my voice cracked and croaked, but cleared it and repeated my appreciation. I wobbly walked to what may have been my room. It was warm and seemed like it was an older child's room now, maybe eight or ten I thought. I once more closed the door behind me and with each door I closed I felt lighter. I was now able to float like the birds of the sky, a destination I had always wanted to be. I continued with the same energy downstairs walking around the bottom floor feeling, smelling and doing my best to remember what was. How life was when I lived here and what my parents were like. I walked into the living room as I noticed the fire place and it was the same one the voice had described to me while stating, it was my fault. I knelt over the fire place as if I was praying, looked into the unlit pit and saw nothing.

No blame, no guilt - just nothing. There was no fire burning and I was no longer sweating. I stood up and looked at the mirror on the wall. I saw myself again and knew who he was. I smiled while I looked at the woman and she smiled back, but when I opened my mouth I said, "It wasn't my fault."

She looked bemused and confused as to what I was talking about, but I just smiled at her. I realised I was alone and may have looked crazy but thanked her for understanding and took my leave closing the final door behind me.

CHAPTER 20

The smell of open wounds and hand sanitizers woke me from my dream. The old man's eyes were still shut and he had one leg outside the covers as if to suggest the temperature was too high. It was quite warm in the room, I admitted silently. There was a window located just above his head but opening it would cause a sudden shock, so I thought against it and rested my head back against the chair feeling my eyes slowly calling it a day.

The sound of the door opening startled me. The nurse burst into the room like there was some sort of emergency. It was loud, rude and to be honest it ticked me off but an apology followed the shock soon after. I gave her a smile to put her worries at ease and she returned it. Noticing that I was not angry, she walked in and was doing some checks on the old man whom was awake by then. He had been awake for a while by the look of it. He probably was watching me sleep, just to make sure I was really there by his side. She looked at his medical records on the tip of the bed and checked the liquid hanging above his head which was almost empty. "Right Mr…" she said a name which I could not repeat. I attempted but it twisted my tongue like a snake wrapped around its prey.

"You are OK to go," she said in a subtle calm voice. "Everything seems fine right now," she continued: "at reception you need to collect an appointment for the next two weeks to come back so we run some more tests and check if your health is on the right track."

The old man nodded to indicate that he understood then looked at me as if to suggest I should go sort that out. I looked back at the nurse and told her "thanks!" She left us to get ourselves in order before returning to double check. The old man looked stronger and the colour in his skin had come back, bright bronze. Maybe he needed some rest and maybe from now on slowing down isn't such a bad thing. I gathered his things and was out the hospital room. The smell was getting to me which burned my nose on the way in and never seemed to leave. The sound of screams still rung my ear as we walked down the corridor. The big green exit sign never seemed more welcoming and my eyes took my attention through a slightly opened door that seemed like it should have been shut. My ears caught the sounds of a woman seated in her bed shouting:

"It hurts! It hurts! It's too hot! Please take it off."

I slowed my walk to almost a standstill but the old man continued without any sudden stop. I began to scan her surroundings to see if I could spot the problem. She was wearing a leg support which was quite large, bright yellow and almost twice her leg size. She must have broken it and kept on trying to pull it off, but strength evaded her as though it hasn't been there in almost twenty years. She screamed and wrestled and if she could use the bad leg to kick she would have. She used everything within reach to get the attention of the already busy nurses who seemed like they didn't care.

I took my gaze from the distressed patient and we reached the reception, collected the appointment and we were soon in a cab heading home.

That night the old man slept like a baby. I was unsettled and I couldn't sleep in peace; I felt that something was bothering me and I found myself getting up several times to check on him and each time I got up he looked at peace.

The morning sun came quickly. The old man was up early as he normally was and we sat by the window watching as the life forces that occupy this planet walked by and sometimes flew by. We spoke about many things before getting up to make breakfast. He didn't eat much, instead he made a joke about watching his weight. Something wasn't right but I laughed regardless the silence after was short.

"Selfishness," he said.

"What about it?" I said, shooting back a swift reply.

"Self-love," he blurted out again

Again I shot back as a batsman would a bowler, "What about it?" I repeated.

"Self-love is very important to one's level of sanity," he began without properly noting whether I was listening. I sat opposite him rocking my head as if I completely understood. "Loving yourself is a powerful thing. You love yourself because of something external. Nicole for an example..." the name sent shivers down my spine.

The words continued to come out of his mouth and I was now following; he mentioned Nicole and my mind drifted in another direction. It wasn't in the directions of the birds nor was it craving for anything from the past. My thoughts lead me to the future. I was no longer scared of the future - I knew what I had to do; I understood my path. Fear was no longer holding me down reminding me of what it was capable of and I was no longer chasing my tail.

The old man stopped talking as he could see I was no longer nodding like a Churchill dog in the back of a car. He kept quiet for a couple minutes and so did I. Perhaps he wanted me to break to depth of the silence but it continued as it created a space for thought.

"What was you thinking about?" he asked.

"The future," I confessed without hesitation.

"It's a wonderful thing isn't it?" he replied.

"Yeah it is," I smiled. My phone rang as a text came through. It was from the lady at the store, Naomi. It read, "*I totally understand, these things happen, I accept your offer and I want you to make it up to me, see you soon.*"

She accepted my offer for a second date. I smiled once more this time revealing my pearl white teeth.

The old man laughed and at the end he said, "It's that lady from the store, isn't it?" I was shocked and amazed that he knew.

"How did you know?" I blurted out.

He finished his giggle then paused and said, "I have eyes in the back of my head." I leaned to the side of the chair and looked at the back of his head. We both laughed and continued to gaze out the window. I looked at him and saw a ticking timer. It was fast approaching zero, the old man was biding his time and I was making sure he was pain free. His time was limited and what a sad day it would be when he too leaves me. I bowed my head discretely to savour the moment.

A couple days had gone past; it was now Thursday and the same old routine continued. The old man slept like a baby and for some reason I couldn't. It would be this evening I would meet up with Naomi which gave me time to prepare. I wasn't to forget Nicole but I was ready to move on. My past was filled with uncertainty, nerves and simply lacked confidence. The voice made me stronger in a sense and weakened me on the other. He taught me things the hard way, I am no longer afraid to be alone or to dream big or to think or criticise. I am free! I was on my knees before I could get up and be counted, and if I'm really honest with myself that was what I really needed. For that I thank him.

The coolness of the floor brought me peace that afternoon, the wooden floor accompanied me as I sat there meditating. I was in a space where my thoughts would never be able to run away or take control. I had it on a short leash, tamed and silenced until called upon. I kept lying there with my eyes closed, feet crossed, fingers connected with a gentle touch. The old man sat by the kitchen counter as his eyes watched me. I could feel his eyes burning in the side of my head.

I was never going to give the thought a chance of rest in the depths of my inner thoughts where I laid my most treasured pictures and memories. I meditated like this for the better part of an hour. I felt good, light and free. I felt like I was able to feel the present, like I was there in the moment, the now, simply being. Who would have thought meditation was so valuable? I opened my eyes and clocked the old man's eyes on me. Just as I suspected he quickly turned his head away in fright. I rose to my feet, stretched it all out and went straight to the bathroom.

The night was cool, not cold, but just chilled enough to wear a thin jacket. I got ready with the thought of what Nicole would have picked out for me. "Why is she still in my head?" I whispered as I wore a black jeans with a white shirt, something simple but casual. The shirt had its top two buttons left open and I felt smooth as I threw my brown jacket over my shoulders. *007* came to mind whilst I cracked a wink in the mirror. I felt like the world's greatest! I looked in the mirror a few more seconds as I looked myself up and down thinking of the beautiful face I saw in the grocery store. She was my opportunity to move on, move on to something great, and find happiness again and perhaps even better than before. I broke eye contact with the man in the mirror and a thought crossed my mind, *you need to slow down* and it echoed in my left ear. I turned around to check what was to be but it wasn't what I thought. I walked out the room and noticed the old man was fast asleep. I smiled whilst grabbing my keys, closed the front door behind me and left.

The taxi pulled up at the restaurant at precisely eight thirty. They do the best chicken in town and it was at the top my list of places to visit. A smile broke out on the corners of my lips as I bowed my head. It wasn't because I was embarrassed, I was merely savouring the moment. A couple weeks ago I never thought I would be so fortunate. I held it closely like it was a secret, I walked into the restaurant where I was greeted by the host. I believe he was the most smartly dressed host I have ever seen. He was donned in a full black suit which on close inspection seemed to be from Italy; *not cheap at all*, I muttered under my breath as he showed me to my seat. I was only to wait a further five minutes before Naomi walked through the door.

She wore an all red dress that almost made me fall off my seat and a black high heels accompanied the dress in a stylish fashion. Her hair puffed out in a neat afro. It looked as though she were the only one that could have pulled it off. Her skin gleamed, beamed and oh my God did it shine! I couldn't stop staring as her eyes searched for mine. The host pointed in my direction and she swiftly followed. My continued gaze watched her as she walked gracefully. Her strides were short and purposeful. It demanded the attention of every diner because with each step she took, the chain of command was hers. Her presence felt strong, back straight and perfection as she was approaching me and I didn't know what to do. Her scent penetrated the depths of my inner senses and I felt as though I had frozen in my seat. She reached close enough to demand the gentleman in me to pull out her chair. I immediately gave her a kiss on both cheeks. Feeling how soft her skin was I got excited.

"How are you?" I asked. She paused without saying a word, it felt like an age but it was only a second or so.

She smiled as the words, "fine, thank you very much," came out. We began to talk and the conversation flowed like a river without barriers. We laughed, joked, flirted and spoke about many things. Her company was out of this world. I found myself comparing her to N…! I caught the words before the name left my lips. It took me longer than usual to eat my food. By this time it was cold but I ate it anyway. Our meal came to a close and as we left the restaurant our night was sealed with a bright smile from the host.

The night was cool, quiet and comforting. Instead of calling a cab, she suggested we walked as she didn't live far away so we took the long way. The street lights accompanied our footsteps. We laughed like kids high on sweets and in no time we reached her front door and almost instantly the school kids giggles came to an end. It was now adults' time. I leant forward, held her chin with the softest of touches and tasted her lips then taking a step back I released and smiled. If I had not held her waist in the process, her legs would have failed her. The moment felt like I had taken her breath away.

"Good night," I uttered, giving no hope anything else. She mirrored my response in the gentlest of voices as her breath returned. I left her half way through her door. I knew the night could have carried on but I wasn't ready for that yet. I walked to the nearest cab station and took a ride back home, well, the old man's place but I still called it home.

I reached home just as the clock struck 11:30pm. The old man wasn't where I had left him in the living room chair. The leg hanging off the bed suggested he had tucked himself in for the night. I was tired after the long day and the alcohol flowed in my system. My legs sluggishly moved me to my room, dropped my clothes and entered the bed. I lay there for a little while looking at the cracks in the ceiling then my eyes got heavy.

"Life," I murmured in a breathless tone.

It was to be a night I would regret for the rest of my life.

CHAPTER 21

The town was peaceful and quiet. Most days it reminded me of a picture I once saw on a post card. It was beautiful, everything I wanted, longed and desired for. Only this time everything was perfect. My family was my reason to keep going. After that date a year ago, we went on several more dates. It was a match made within the heavens, crafted and designed by the universe of gods. We went on to have a beautiful son; his first birthday comes next month. Every time I look at him I see pure hope. Strength was always what I lacked and now I have it in him, my only aim is to maintain it. If not for me it has to be for my son.

We had to move out of the city as it was damaging our mental state and the desire for a new start was more appealing. Now we live in a small town out in the country side. The simplest of things is what we desire now. Everyone greets each other, something I had never seen before coming from London. Naomi had sold her shop so we had a lot more money to create the dream we now share. She is absolute gold. I had told her about all the struggles I had gone through, the ups and downs, mostly downs, but that did not scare her off. Actually if anything it made her love me more. You see, if there was one thing I had learned from all this is at any one moment life can make you feel like you are winning, like you have everything, like you have all the time in the world, everyone around you that loves you and yet round the corner a whole different story is waiting for you. Struggles and challenges. Savour moments and be present when all is well.

Life's too short to waste it, I noted as I walked down this street. It smelled of freshly baked bread, the steam danced atop as the baker lay it to settle. The sun bathed my skin as a shadow accompanied me. I was on my usual morning stroll. Every morning I would walk down to this lake, it wasn't nothing special, nothing like the size you could swim in but for some reason it was special to me. Every morning without fail I would walk down to this lake, stand over it, gazing without distraction, a face would always look back at me. This time it was someone recognisable, this time I saw me and I looked good, loved and wanted around. I was the man I had always wanted to become, the old man was my saviour but it needed to come from within and eventually come out. The lake also revealed life to me; it's not just a pond filled with life swimming around neither is it just a place where people ignore the signs and feed the fish anyway. It's a place of calm, the little fish swam without care or responsibility. The old man and his dog were gone, *he died in his bed as peaceful as ever, one leg hanging off the bed just as he liked to sleep, his dog moved with us shortly after that and died of old age a couple months ago, he was my living legend.* What he left behind was beyond what any price could attain. The wind blew a gust of dust causing me to close my eyes and at that moment I uttered, "I miss you, I wish things could have been different, but I know your presence and energy is with me."

My eyes felt comfortable enough to unseal. I felt a small figure by my side; it was a little girl. She stared out into the water as if she was thinking of going for a swim. I turned my head and she didn't move. She had a great sensation of heat coming from her. It was quite overwhelming so I took a step back, she looked at me and I at her.

"What are you doing?" she enquired. I paused, I didn't know how to answer her. She wasn't frightening or intimidating. She was just there doing what I was doing, wondering as I wondered. She must of been no older than nine. *Should I give her the truth or should I tell her that the reason why I come to this lake every morning is to protect the demons that may come back, or tell her that I was once weaker than she could imagine, or should I just walk away in the shadows of the mummy strollers like a James bond film?*

The temperature in my chest began to rise and the beat sounded like a Nyabinghi drum that kept on playing. I began to recognise it and I moved with it. My feet didn't move but my soul connected with it and it became my sanctuary. What seemed like a long time was less than a minute as I noticed the mummy and stroller crew was still walking past and had only reached a few meters away.

I finally opened my jaws and said, "A place I can also escape to."

"Escape?" she asked as she stretched the word, confused as if she knew it was a place that held people captive. I wondered if I should continue. *Should I tell her the reason I chose this lake when there are nicer lakes less than a stone throw away?* "When my mummy takes me to the park I see you standing here all the time and I say to my mummy, 'There's that man again.'"

I looked at her and smiled. "This pond gives me a sense of control," I uttered as if I was speaking to an adult. "When I stare at the water my mind jumps off into the most beautiful place you could ever imagine." She looked at me with a smile that was missing a few teeth.

"Does this place have sweets and ice creams?" I also smiled.

"Yes! It does," I replied. "This place is where everyone is happy, there is no fear, worries or problems."

"That sounds like heaven," she concluded.

"Something like that," I replied and pointed. "Look, your mummy is calling you." "Same time tomorrow?" she asked. I almost burst out into an uncontrollable laughter. "Maybe," I said in response and waved goodbye.

An hour or so had passed and Naomi would be wondering if I had ran away, so without any further meditation I left the park. The walk back home was only fifteen minutes so it took no time. The sun glared in my eyes as a car drove past, leaving me stunned. A soft, subtle, almost new and unrecognisable voice said, "Hey, how are you?"

I replied, "Hi, I'm great," then the voice in my head vanished. I walked through the door. Naomi was on the couch reading a book and beside her was Dillion in his rocker. "DADDA!" is what we heard, more so me than Naomi. I think she was jealous that he called me first but we looked at each other with amazement plastered on our faces and smiles painted on our lips. We screamed, scaring him in the process. It was his first words!

I shouted, "Aww Dillion," as we scrambled to cuddle him. His legs shook, kicked and slapped as if he was a karate master fighting several opponents. The rocker rocked him gently with excitement. I knelt before him and as he held my finger. I looked into his eyes for a brief moment, and just as tears formed, I kissed him.